(Latt

Adrienne Thompson

Pink Cashmere Publishing, LLC

Arkansas, USA

Cover art by AA Thompson (thompson9699@gmail.com)

Printed in the United States of America

First Printing 2016

ISBN: 0-9971461-4-1
ISBN-13: 978-0-9971461-4-1

Dear Lord, thank You so much for my life, my family, and my Jesus. In all I do, I truly seek to glorify You.

To my readers: I cannot thank you enough for your support. God bless.

"Do not arouse or awaken love until it so desires."
Song of Songs 3:5 NIV

Soundtrack:

"I Get Lonely" *Janet Jackson featuring Blackstreet*

"Something in the Past" *Jesse Powell*

"Here I Go Again" *Glenn Jones*

"How You Gonna Act Like That" *Tyrese*

"Think It Over" *Angie Stone*

"Begin Again" *Angie Stone featuring Dave Hollister*

"Family Affair" *Sly & The Family Stone*

"Lately" *Jodeci*

"Prior to You" *Tyrese featuring Tank*

"Love Under New Management" *Miki Howard*

"What Am I Gonna Do" *Tyrese*

"Real Life" *The Weeknd*

"Hey Daddy" *Usher*

"Reunion" *Maxwell*

"Another Round" *Jaheim*

"Smooth Criminal" *Michael Jackson*

"Bloodstream" *Stateless*

"Matrimony: Maybe You" *Maxwell*

"You" *Jesse Powell*

"...Til The Cops Come Knockin'" *Maxwell*

This soundtrack is available on YouTube.

Prologue

Rochelle
Then…

I stood in a room crammed full of girls situated in lines of ten. The vast majority were teenagers or had just transitioned from teenagers to young adults. Taut bodies and long hair that may or may not have naturally grown from their heads were abundant, as was dewy skin and heavy make-up. They were beautiful, every man's fantasy, and there I stood among them, much older than most of them at thirty-three years old, but no one could tell thanks to excellent genes and melanin. My tiny waist and curvy everything else were the assets that got me there. I hoped those same assets would ensure I would become one of the chosen ones.

I stood with my head held high, smiled brightly, stuck my ample chest out, and silently prayed that he'd like what he saw, that he'd see me and instantly decide I had the "it" factor.

"Here he comes," a girl whispered, sending ripples of the same words throughout the room. I panicked a little, tried to stand taller. Then I started wondering if I had anything in my teeth. Was my lipstick smeared? Was my smile bright enough or too bright? Was I standing there looking like The Joker? Would he think I was crazy, too enthusiastic?

He entered the stuffy room, looking even more handsome than when I'd seen him in the past. There was a softness to his looks; he was more pretty boy than rugged. His brown eyes, which had always looked a little sad to me, swept over the room as he quickly assessed each girl. His thick eyebrows furrowed as he focused on a girl who sadly was not me. I kept wearing that smile, though, and kept silently praying. Five girls, that was how many would be chosen. So I still stood a chance... I hoped.

He whispered something in her ear, and she giggled before stepping out of her line and being escorted out of the room by one of the burly men who stood on either side of the door. I dropped my smile for a split second and released a quick breath before smiling again. He moved throughout the room slowly, chose another girl. This one squealed with delight before virtually bouncing out of the room. Then a third girl was chosen... then a fourth, and my spirits dropped a few notches with each choice. The chosen were all very young, very thin, and very European-looking. There I stood with the curves of a woman my age, thick lips, a wide nose, and sun-kissed brown skin, and the reality that I was obviously not what he was looking for hit me full force, and at the same time, I dropped the smile and let my shoulders slump. I stopped arching my back and lowered my breasts, and by the time he made it to my row, I had a bit of an attitude.

He walked down the row, stopped at the girl next to me, and I inadvertently rolled my eyes. She was a cookie-cutter version of the other girls—tall, lean, and light, bright, damn near white. I softly scoffed when he leaned in and whispered in her ear. Out of the corner of my eye, I saw his head snap up and in my direction. His soft eyes met mine, and something inside of me melted a bit. "Did you say something?" he asked.

His voice.

I'd heard it before, knew it well, but there in the same room with me, it was so soft, so gentle, so... sexy. I was left speechless.

"Okay," he said. "Let's try this: what's your name?"

"Chelly," I said, giving him my self-assigned professional name.

"Chelly. I like that." He left the girl next to me and stood directly in front of me, a couple of inches taller than me in my uncomfortable heels. I stared at him against my will, and my eyes took in those sad brown eyes, smooth tan skin that boasted his half-black, half-Puerto Rican heritage, and thin lips that I already knew would eventually part into a pristine white smile. No facial hair. He was a beautiful man, more beautiful than any woman I'd ever seen. He leaned in close to my ear; minty breath brushed my skin as he whispered, "I think we'd go good together. You?"

I nodded, and instead of directing me toward one of the guys by the door, he took my hand and escorted me himself. Several pairs of jealous eyes followed us out of the room.

1

"I Get Lonely"

Rochelle
Now…

I was so tired of sleeping alone I could scream. I mean, I talked a good game about how the last thing I wanted was the trouble of having a man, but truthfully, being a single mother was for the birds. Don't get me wrong, I loved my son and I loved being his mother when he was in his right mind. But any woman who says she'd prefer to do it alone is either lying or a straight-up fool in my opinion. What woman in her right mind would actually prefer to make every single decision and pay every bill and sign every note and attend every school function… alone? Not me, not really. There had been so many times in the past fifteen years that I wished someone would take up some of the slack for me, make one or two of the decisions, write a check, pick up some take-out—something! But I was alone in this, had been alone since the day he was born. Hell, his daddy wasn't even around for the birth.

Now, I'd never been a complete fool. Yes, I fell in love with a deadbeat, but I also made sure he took care of what was his, so I'd been getting child support all those years. We lived comfortably, and if I really wanted to, I could've quit my job. But what would be worse than sleeping alone would be spending every day—day in and day out—alone in my house. I would've rather worked somewhere, *anywhere*, than stayed in that house alone day in and day out. So I worked, took care of my son, went to church, cooked meals (sort of), and climbed into my bed… alone.

And I was so tired of it.

Okay, I guess I need to admit that my being alone was kind of my fault. At fifty, I still had a good body and face, and plenty of men in my backwater hometown had hit on me, some single and some definitely *not* single. But I just wasn't attracted to any of them—not one. I had a type, and none of them fit my type. But then again, the one man who *did* fit my type got me pregnant and dumped me as soon as I told him, because he wasn't "ready." Hell, neither was I, but I *got* ready because that's what grown folks do. They see a responsibility in front of them and they deal with it, not run away from it. Well my Jesse Owens-like baby daddy took off and didn't look back.

Lowdown, dirty…

Oh, how I hated that man! Anyway, I knew I needed to figure something out. I needed to lower my standards or something. I needed and wanted a man. I just had no idea what to do about it.

2

"Something in the Past"

I was in a bad mood when I made it to work that morning, and I don't even know why. It wasn't as if something different had happened. I woke up on my side of the bed, had breakfast with my largely mute son. Tried not to commit an arrestable offense when he said something smart to me in response to a question I asked in the car. Prayed to sweet Jesus to keep me from killing him as I drove to work. Same thing, another day. Absolutely nothing new. But when I stepped into the room in Hyacinth Manor that served as a break room, I was hit with an overwhelming feeling of I-don't-wanna-be-here-or-have-to-deal-with-these-people-today. And I cannot tell you why. Yes, Ms. Dorcas was nosy and Dee Dee was ditzy and Ms. Rosa was a know-it-all (and she was always right), but I was used to all of that, and besides, Ms. Rosa wasn't even there. Something just wasn't right with me that day.

"Girl, what's wrong with you?" Ms. Dorcas asked as I slumped into a chair at the table and dropped my purse on the floor beside me.

"Nothing, why?" I replied a little more defensively than I'd intended.

She adjusted that red wig of hers and sat across from me. "You look like you are two seconds from putting your foot up someone's behind. Who spit in your coffee this morning?"

"No one—Justin, I guess. He decided to mouth off on the way to school."

"Lord, that boy again?"

I nodded, decided no good would come of me admitting I was also lonely and stressed out from the responsibilities of my life.

"Humph, you been taking him to church? Making sure he hears the word?"

"I take him, but I can't make him listen. I mean, he can sit there but I have no idea what's on his mind."

"He needs his daddy."

I worked really hard not to roll my eyes and wished I hadn't confided in her. She always took the conversation there when we talked about Justin. "Ms. Dorcas—"

"My Sammy wasn't worth a plum nickel, but just the fact that he was there in the house and owned a whole lotta thick leather belts kept my boys in line. Listen to me because I know what I'm talking about. That boy needs his daddy."

I sighed. "Well, I don't know what I can do about that short of pointing a gun at the man's head and making him come be his daddy, Ms. Dorcas. He's not in Justin's life by choice."

"Go get him another one. Rochelle, you are a beautiful woman, and honey, I wish you could take them hips off and let me borrow them for just a couple of hours. Shoot, if I was built like you, I would do some damage!"

I smiled and felt some of the tension I'd carried into the building leave me. "Ms. Dorcas, you're a mess."

"I'm serious! Girl, go get you a husband, someone who can be a father to that boy. He's too handsome and smart to be getting on the wrong track, but that's exactly what he's gonna keep doing without some type of father figure in his life."

"Ms. Dorcas, you act like men are just standing on the side of the street, holding up signs begging for a wife. This is a small town. Half the men are married, and the ones that ain't married are either gay or ugly. And I don't do the online thing. I'm not trying to get catfished."

"Cat what?"

I chuckled. "Being catfished is not a good thing, Ms. Dorcas. I mean, short of moving, I don't know what to do. And I don't want to move, because my mom and dad are here and they're all the help I have. If it wasn't for them helping me with Justin, I would've lost it long ago."

"Well, Vance Washington still lives here, and he's still single, and he's still got it bad for you."

I shook my head. "Don't go there, Ms. Dorcas."

"What?" she said, innocently.

"Been there, tried that. It didn't work out. He's just not my type."

"So, tall, dark, and fine ain't your type?"

"Tall, dark, fine with a crazy ex-wife ain't my type."

"That girl moved a year ago. You better get your head on straight and give that man a chance. He makes good money, too. Could help you with a bill or two. Shoot, you give him a chance and you just might fall in love."

With that, she stood from the table, rubbed her lower back, and walked her tiny frame out the door.

***

We had a couple with a reservation to arrive at the manor that day, and since Ms. Rosa was away visiting her son, everything fell on me to do. I was actually relieved because it took my mind off of my woes, and thankfully, Ms. Dorcas was too busy in the kitchen to get in my business the rest of that day. Since Rosa liked for the staff to have dinner with guests every evening if at all possible, I had my mother pick Justin up from school. She quickly offered to let him spend the night which was great since I'd also have to spend the night at the manor. In the past, Justin would stay at the manor with me, but I have to admit that I was relieved not to have to spend the evening with him or his smart mouth. And since he seemed to know how to respect my parents, I knew he wouldn't give them any trouble.

I was the sounding board for his anger, I suppose, because I was there all the time and always had been. I wondered if he'd be that angry at his father given the chance to confront him. Then again, I knew the answer to that. I knew he was angry at him for not making him a part of his world and for not taking the time to be a father to him. As much as he seemed to dislike me as of late, his feelings for his father were more intense and much more hostile. I wished there was something I could do to fix things. Actually, I wished I could go back in time and pick him a better father, but he wouldn't be the taller-than-me, handsome combination of me and his wayward father if he had a different sperm donor. Hell, to be honest, the boy looked almost exactly like the man.

After dinner with the couple, who Rosa had instructed me to put in Room Six, I sat at my desk in my tiny office and tried to gather myself enough to climb the stairs and go to bed. Before I knew it, I'd drifted off to sleep with my head resting on my old wooden desk.

"You know why I chose you?" he asked as I sat next to him in the back of a limousine with an interior that smelled of cherries and the marijuana he was known to partake of.

I shook my head, feeling too shy to be a fully grown woman.

"There's something special about you. You stood up there with your fine self and acted like you really didn't care about any of this, or about me. Man, I like that."

"Actually, I was over you picking those light-skinned skeletons."

He looked at me, furrowed his brow, and then released a scoff that quickly turned into laughter. "Damn, okay. Tell me how you really feel, Chelly. I like 'em thick like you, too, you know?"

I shrugged.

"You're so different from most of the girls I spend time with. You're more mature."

Probably because I'm a grown woman and not a little girl, I thought, but I said, "Oh, really?"

"Truly."

He was so odd. Soft spoken but full of confidence, and somehow, there was an edge to him that I couldn't explain. He was a pretty man, but something underneath was rugged, unrefined, and I think that was what really attracted me to him.

"I want you to hang with me," he said as he licked his barely-there lips. That, I didn't like. I preferred thick lips on a man.

I crossed my legs, felt the flirt inside of me begin to break forth. "I thought we were already hanging."

"I mean, when this night is over, I want you to stay with me. Be my number one."

I rolled my neck as I turned to fully face him. "Being number one means there's a two, three, or even a four out there somewhere. I don't play that. And besides, you don't know me to be trying to make me your number anything."

He nodded and held up his hands. "Okay, Chelly, I hear you. How about this? Let's see where tonight takes us, okay? If it takes us to a place we don't want to come back from, so be it."

Against my better judgement, my response was, "Okay."

My head snapped up, and I almost fell out of my chair as I became aware of my surroundings. That dream was much more than a dream. It was a memory—one that made my heart race and sent a surge of heat to the core of my body. His face, his voice, his *everything* made me realize just how long it had been, just how much I missed being with a man, and just how much I wanted to be with one again. Fifteen years is a long time for anyone to be alone.

I shook the memories and empty desires off, stood from the chair, and stretched my legs before grabbing my purse and heading upstairs with the master key in hand. I passed by Room Ten, just as I had so many times when I spent the night at the manor. Shoot, to be honest, I was scared of the legendary "fall in love" room. But for a brief second that evening, I thought about spending the night in there. Then I found my mind again and decided I wasn't that desperate. I would get over these feelings. I had to, because loving a man brought nothing but trouble. At least that had been my experience. Love was a joke, a cruel one.

I finally made it to my destination, good old Room Two, and quickly crawled into bed. Thankfully, no dreams invaded my sleep for the rest of the night.

3

"Here I Go Again"

I ran home for a little while the next morning to be greeted with a letter from *him* stashed amongst the mail in my mailbox. He'd taken to writing little letters to Justin off and on over the past five or six years. I usually read them and then threw them away. The last thing my son needed was a bunch of false promises and false hope from that man. Things would be better if his father didn't have the chance to disappoint him as I knew he would. He wasn't a good man and certainly not father material. He was living life in the fast lane when I met him, and as far as I could see, that hadn't changed, no matter what he put in those letters. He was the same sorry excuse for a man he was fifteen years ago. I was sure of that.

After sifting through bills and catalogs, I picked up the envelope with his sloppy handwriting on the front—his California address in the top left hand corner. Seeing his name made my stomach tie itself up in knots. I told myself for the millionth time that it was a mistake to give him my address. Then I reminded myself that I'd had to disclose my address to the courts in order to receive child support, and if his trifling behind wasn't going to step up and physically help me with Justin, he for darn sure was going to help me financially.

There was a visitation schedule put in place when Justin was a baby, too, but he'd never bothered following it. He hadn't seen him since he was born except for a couple of pictures I sent him before I realized he didn't care. And I wasn't even sure he ever received them since I never heard back from him about them.

I balled the unopened letter up and threw it into the trash can in my bedroom. Then I took a shower, dressed, and returned to work.

***

The guests didn't come out of their room for breakfast, thank goodness, because after the dream and the letter and the fact that my life still sucked, I wasn't in any mood to smile and invite them to take a stroll on the property or anything of the sort. To be honest, I really wasn't fit to spend time around other adults at all, so I was glad my two co-workers were too busy to seek me out.

As if the fact that I was already in a funk wasn't enough, I received a phone call that sent me from a little down to completely upset. I knew it was trouble when I saw a number that I was unfortunately becoming very familiar with.

"Hello?" I silently prayed they'd misdialed or had the wrong number—*anything*.

"Ms. Warrior, please."

Damn.

"This is she," I said through a sigh.

"Hi, Ms. Warrior. This is Lettie Barnes up here at the junior high school?" she said as if I could've possibly mistaken her painfully nasal voice for anyone else's.

"Yes, what's going on?" I asked, although a huge part of me really didn't want to know.

"There's been an incident and—"

"An incident? A fight? Has Justin been in a fight?"

"No, ma'am. He's had a run-in with one of his teachers."

I closed my eyes and released another sigh. "A run-in? Um... on my way right now."

I quickly drove to the neighboring town, which housed the junior high school, and entered the office to see my boy sitting in a corner with his arms folded over his chest and a look that would kill in his eyes, those eyes he shared with his doggone father. I stood in front of him, and said, "What's going on, Justin?" as calmly as I could.

"Didn't they tell you already?" he asked in a tone that was laced with a little too much attitude for someone who was in trouble.

"What?" I almost forgot where I was for a second, but lucky for both of us, the principal, one Mr. Vance Washington, greeted us and then ushered us into his office. Well, he ushered *me* into his office while Justin dragged his feet and joined us a full minute after both me and Vance were already seated.

Vance's dark eyes swept over my body as he said, "It's good to see you, Rochelle. Even under these circumstances."

I nodded, gave him a tense smile.

He was tall, dark, and fine just like Ms. Dorcas said, and most of the single women in our little town had been after him for a long time. He was my age and had a good job and a kind heart. We dated on and off for a full year and he even proposed. I was still thinking about taking him up on his offer when his ex took a bat and busted my windshield. That little incident, coupled with the fact that I didn't even really love him, prompted me to end things. Five years had passed, but Ms. Dorcas was right. I could tell at that moment that he still liked me, maybe even loved me. And that made this whole situation even more uncomfortable for me. I was going to give Justin a few pieces of my mind when I got him alone for putting me in front of a man whose heart I had probably broken.

When Justin finally slumped into the chair next to mine, Vance said, "Justin, as I told you before your mother arrived, I am shocked about what happened today."

Justin shrugged.

I clasped my hands in my lap. "That's all you got to say? *Nothing*? I left my job and you have nothing to say for yourself? No explanation, Justin?"

"It ain't like you got a real job. You living off my child support, so it don't matter that you had to leave."

Oh, sweet Jesus, Mary, and Joseph! This little Negro done lost his entire, complete, whole, total, utter mind talking to me like this! "What?!" I shouted before I could stop myself. Then I saw myself jump to my feet. I must've been looking real crazy, too, because the expression on Justin's face softened. He even looked halfway scared.

"Ma'am?" His voice was much less hostile.

"I said, *what*? What did you just say to me?"

"Nothing."

I reclaimed my seat. "That's what I thought. Now, what did you do?"

He glanced at me. "Ms. Kendall called me out about the homework and I told her I didn't do her stupid homework and I ain't *gon'* do it. Crap's too easy."

I kept my eyes on him, waiting on the rest, because I knew there had to be more.

"And then she handed me a detention slip and I balled it up and threw it at her... and it hit her."

"Ro—Ms. Warrior, this is serious, and what Justin did could've been seen as assault. Luckily, I was able to talk Ms. Kendall down, but he will have to be disciplined for his actions," Vance said.

I nodded. "Of course, and I am so sorry about this. Once I get Justin home, I will get to the bottom of his behavior, because he knows better." I cut my eyes at Justin. "What's his punishment?"

"He's being sent home for three days."

"Three days?! I mean, okay... um, I see." I glanced over at Justin whose eyes were glued to the floor. "Well, again, I'm sorry. Please give my apologies to Ms. Kendall and let her know Justin will be apologizing in front of the entire class when he's allowed to return to school."

Justin's head jerked up and he looked at me. I gave him *the eye* and he dropped his gaze again.

I stood and proffered Vance my hand.

He took it in his, held onto it a little too long. "I sure will let her know." He locked eyes with mine as I slipped my hand out of his. Then I left with my son in tow.

4

"How You Gonna Act Like That"

I drove home in silence, felt Justin staring at me for most of the ride, but refused to look at him. I drove his behind straight to my mother's house, parked in the driveway, and pressed the button to unlock the doors. I glanced over at him to see him staring at me, and his eyes bore the same sadness that was always in his father's eyes. That sadness fooled me all those years ago. That wasn't about to happen again. "I need to go back to my *fake* job and I'll be there all night. Tell Grandma I need you to spend the night again. I'll go by the house and bring you some more clothes. We'll talk about this later, because I don't wanna say something crazy to you right now."

"Sorry, Mama," he mumbled.

"Sorry for what? Acting a fool with your teacher or talking crazy to me?"

"Both."

I dropped my hands from the steering wheel. "Why'd you do it? Have I not taught you to respect adults, especially teachers?"

He shrugged.

"Un-uh. Go on in the house, Justin. I don't have time to play the shoulder game with you. Just go on inside. When you're ready to use your words, call me."

"I just don't like her, and her class is stupid."

I didn't like her, either. She always had a nasty attitude from the time we were in high school together. I wasn't surprised Justin disliked her. Wouldn't have been surprised if half of the student body hated her, but I couldn't tell him that. "Where is it written that you have to like your teachers or their classes? Who told you that, because it's a lie. Look, Justin, school is your training ground. You might graduate and go out in the world and work for someone you don't like, and acting a fool with them will get you nowhere but in the unemployment line."

He remained silent.

"Or maybe you'll end up working for yourself—"

With lifted eyebrows and curiosity in his eyes, he interrupted me by saying, "Like my dad?"

I was so taken aback that I actually flinched a little. "Y-yes, like your dad. Look, all I'm saying is, no matter your line of work, you have to know how to treat people. Treat them the way you want to be treated no matter how you feel about them."

"Yes, ma'am. I understand. I wonder what he'd think of me if he saw me."

I frowned slightly. "Who?"

"My dad."

I cleared my throat. Where in the world were these questions coming from? "He'd... he'd be proud of the boy you're growing up to be, but disappointed in your behavior today and the attitude you take with me from time to time."

"I'm disappointed in *his* behavior."

We both fell silent.

I reached over and gently rubbed his cheek. "I love you, and I know it's hard being a teenager and not having your father around. I picked him, so I apologize for that, but Justin Xavier Warrior, if you *ever* fix your mouth to disrespect me the way you did in Mr. Washington's office again, they're gonna have to put me in jail. Let that be the last time you mouth off at me. You've obviously mistaken my kindness for weakness. I love you, and I understand this is a difficult time in your life, but don't you ever disrespect me again. You hear me?"

He dropped his eyes. "Yes, ma'am. I'm sorry."

"Apology accepted."

"Mama... can I ask you something?"

"Yeah, baby?"

"You still like Mr. Washington?"

"What?" *What's with this kid today? Sheesh!*

"I remember y'all used to like each other, used to go on dates and stuff. You still like him?"

"I... don't know, Justin. Why?"

"He's cool. He didn't talk crazy to me or nothing when he took me to his office. I like him." And with that, he climbed out of my car and walked up my parents' gravel driveway to their white frame house.

***

17

He literally took my breath away the first time he kissed me, I mean, really kissed me. It wasn't like it was my first kiss or my first anything else with a man, but I'd never felt anything so gentle, yet so urgent, before in my life.

His hands were everywhere.

So were mine.

He felt good, like a warm blanket in winter. We'd been together for a week getting to know each other, had been nearly inseparable, and I could honestly say I was the happiest I'd ever been in my life. Being in his life, on his arm, was like a fantasy. A fantasy laced with expensive weed and liquor. It was reckless, and I suppose I liked that part of it, too.

My mind was in a haze as he kissed and caressed his way up and down my body. I knew better. Knew I should've stopped him. Knew this wasn't right and that if I let it happen, I would be no better than the other girls, the hangers-on and wannabes. But I was intoxicated by him and the chemicals that were in my body, high as a kite on lust and desire, and he was my drug of choice. We did it in the back of his limo, which made it even more exciting for me. Knowing the partition was down and that the driver could hear and see, even smell us, fueled my desire for him and his love. His love went down smooth, like the bottle of expensive rum we'd shared earlier that night, and it was just as inebriating.

When it was over, reality and reason found their way back into my brain, and I wondered if he was going to kick me out of the parked limo whose windows we'd successfully steamed up. Instead, he lit a big blunt, puffed on it, and passed it to me. Then we rode to his place, where our private party lasted all night long.

I woke up tangled in sweat-drenched sheets, the familiar powder blue decor of Room Two surrounding me. I was so groggy and so, well... hot and bothered, that I barely remember climbing out of bed and grabbing my master key. What I do remember very vividly is waking up the next morning in Room Ten.

5

"Think it Over"

What the hell have I done?

That was my first thought upon awakening the next morning.

Why was I in that room? How'd I get there?

It was the last place I wanted to be. As a matter of fact, I hated even peeking into that room to check on guests. I hated passing it when I walked down the hall. I hated the fact that it even existed. Yes, I told guests it was the best room in the house, but I meant for them. Not for me.

Never for me.

So what on God's green, luscious Earth was I doing there?

Then I remembered the dream—him and me, the passion, my past stupidity. And I realized it had finally become too much for me. Years of remembering the last man I'd slept with had taken the rational part of my brain, and evidently, eviscerated it, leaving me dumb enough to venture into that room and sleep in that bed in hopes of—what? Falling in love? And with who? Vance?

Then a thought hit me. Why not Vance? He was handsome enough. Not exactly my type, but did that really matter at this point? And Justin liked him. Maybe he'd even listen to him. Maybe we could become a family. But then there was Starla, crazy-ass Starla—who, though they'd been apart for years, just couldn't let go. But Ms.

Dorcas said she'd moved, and I hadn't heard of any more of her shenanigans in a while, so maybe... just maybe.

At the very least I could test out the room, see if the legend was true or if it was purely coincidental that people who stayed in Room Ten fell in love shortly thereafter. I mean, surely it was a hoax. After all, it took good old August Donovan three years to fall in love after staying in that room. That alone proved the logic to be faulty.

But, he *did* fall in love, and when he fell, he *fell*, had the pretty wife and new life to prove it. Would the same happen to me? How long would it take? Surely not three years! *Oh, Lord, let it work quicker for me,* I softly prayed, and then I pinched myself, yelped, and told myself to snap out of it! I didn't want to fall in love ever again... right?

But as hard as I tried to pretend I didn't care about the legend of the room or falling in love, I just couldn't shake this weird feeling. I spent the day working—making things comfortable for our guests, accepting phone calls from past guests seeking reservations, making arrangements for the leaves to be raked since our groundskeeper left us behind when he got married. But always at the back of my mind was the possibility of love and what it could mean for me and for Justin. Maybe being in love would make me a better mother, dilute some of my anger. Maybe Justin would see me in a new light if I was happier. Maybe—

"Did someone sleep in Room Ten last night?" Dee Dee, our one and only housekeeper, asked.

My head snapped up from the paperwork on my desk. "W-what?"

She placed her meaty hands on her extra wide hips and repeated herself. "Did someone sleep in Room Ten last night?"

I frowned slightly, hid my eyes from her. "Of course not. You know only Ms. Rosa can assign that room to guests. Why?"

"I was doing my daily rounds, you know, checking the rooms and stuff, and I noticed the bed isn't made up the way I make it up."

"Really? Maybe one of our guests got lost and stumbled into there."

She seemed to think about my suggestion for a moment and then said, "But the door was locked."

"Hmmm, I don't know, Dee Dee. Maybe you're just mistaken about the bed."

"Maybe. I *have* been tired lately. Me and Hudson been fighting a lot." She took a seat across from my desk, and I breathed a sigh of relief. The last thing I wanted to do was explain why I, the self-professed queen of singlehood, had spent the night in that room.

"What's going on now? He quit another good job?"

"Yeah, girl! How'd you know?"

Because that's always what it is with you two. "Lucky guess."

"Well, like my cousin Gladys Knight says, I'm just trying to keep on keeping on, but it's hard with a man like him, you know? Girl, he had a good job at the donut factory over in New Freedom, benefits and everything, and then he quit last week because there weren't enough black people in management. I told him that was the craziest thing I'd ever heard in my life. Hell, if he'd stayed, *he* could've become a manager!"

I chuckled and listened as she went on and on, complaining about her man and quoting a myriad of fake cousins. I was glad for the distraction.

***

I decided to go with it, to test out the power of the room, and if it happened, if I fell in love, then so be it. So at the time I would've picked Justin up had he not been suspended, I headed to the school anyway, into the building, and into Vance's office to find the secretary's desk unmanned. I peeped around the corner into his door to see him in at his desk busily filling out paperwork. I knocked on the door facing and cleared my throat.

His eyes lit up when he looked up and saw me. He smiled, stood from his desk. "Rochelle—Ms. Warrior, I wasn't expecting you. Uh… have a seat."

"Sorry to interrupt you. Um, were you busy?"

He quickly shook his head as I settled into the seat I'd occupied the day before. "No, not at all. Just going over some paperwork, but it can wait. What's on your mind? Did you want to discuss what happened with Justin yesterday?"

I folded my hands in my lap, suddenly feeling foolish for being there, but it was too late. I knew I may as well follow through with this ridiculous plan. "Um, Vance… I've been thinking a lot about the past here lately."

"Really? What part of the past?"

"*Our* past. I was thinking that things were good for the most part.

Would you agree with that?"

He leaned forward, wearing a wide smile. "Our time together was one of the best periods of my life, Rochelle, and I have to admit that I've missed you a lot. I know I've said it before, but I apologize for what Starla did."

"I know, and I realize it wasn't your fault. I just didn't want to have to deal with the drama. I still don't."

"Rochelle, as much as I'm enjoying this walk down memory lane and just being able to sit here and look into your lovely face, I need to know—what are you saying to me right now?"

"I'm saying I'd like to try again. I mean, I'm not seeing anyone. Are you?"

"Well, if I understand you correctly, I think I'm about to be seeing you again."

I gave him a smile, stood from my seat. "Well, I guess I'll be in touch, then."

6

"Begin Again"

There were times when I would just sit and stare at him while he slept. I wished I really understood him, but he was a conundrum to me. I often wondered how someone could be so gentle yet passionate at the same time. Hardworking, but irresponsible. We spent so many days and countless hours in bed, high or drunk. He was a successful man, so I never really understood why he lived so recklessly or what pain he was trying to numb. As for me, I just wanted to forget that I was in my thirties and had never finished anything. I was a serial starter. I jumped from thing to thing like a grasshopper. Never finished college or beauty school. Took a few dance classes but decided that wasn't for me. Cooking classes were a bust, too. I was good at sewing but didn't have the passion to pursue a career in fashion. My style was different and so was my thinking, but being different had gotten me nowhere.

There I was, a fully grown woman with lots of dreams but no direction. I hadn't accomplished anything except for being his woman—a position I'd held for nearly a year, the longest I'd held any position, and I was good at it, too. Very good. It was almost as if I was made just for him.

In that year that was hazy for me at best, I had grown to love the life we had together. And I had also grown to love him. Told him every time he put it on me, but he never spoke those words to me until one night when we were in some hotel room in some city. I was curled up tightly in his arms, we had just made love, and he very softly whispered in my ear, "Love you, Chelly."

I first wondered whether it was the weed or maybe the rum talking, but nevertheless, I replied in kind. "I love you, too."

That dream didn't get me hot and bothered, it actually pissed me off. Love? Really? Since when did overindulgence and wild sex equal love? What in the world was my subconscious mind trying to do? Convince me that what I thought I felt all those years ago was really love? Make me believe the king of lies had meant what he said? Did my mind not know I'd hit the big five-o, that I was not a fool anymore?

"You wanna be in love so bad?" I muttered to myself as I reached over on the bedside table in Room Two. "All right, let's do this."

I dialed his number, waited to hear his groggy, "hello?" and then I said, "Good morning, Vance. I'm so sorry to call you this early, but I woke up with you on my mind."

It was kind of true.

"Really?" His voice had perked up considerably.

"Yes, um... I don't want to hold you long, but would you like to do lunch today? You can eat with me here at the manor if you'd like."

"I'd love that, Rochelle."

"Great. See you around noon, then?"

"Definitely."

We said our goodbyes, and then I walked over to the dresser mirror and declared, "You wanna be in love? Well, let's fall the hell in love, then!"

***

Lunch with Vance was nice. No sparks flew and my heart didn't race, but it was nice to be with him and listen to him talk about his day. We had lunch on the back patio instead of in the dining room with the guests, so we had a bit of privacy and that was a good thing. The last thing I needed was Ms. Dorcas sticking her head out of the kitchen every other minute trying to see what we were talking about. She was Vance's biggest cheerleader, and knowing her, she'd be trying to marry us off before the end of the meal.

"Here I am, rambling on about fire drills and parent-teacher conferences coming up, and I haven't even asked you about your day. How's it been so far?" he asked.

I gave him a smile, thought back to all the times we spent together in the past. Just as he was on this day, he was always considerate and easy on the eyes. I had to wonder what about him made me back away besides Starla, because I dealt with crazy women in my relationship with Justin's father all the time and they didn't deter me a bit. But then again, I was crazy in love with him, and I never wanted to feel like that again. That level of lack of control over my own emotions was scary. But sitting there with Vance, I could see where we could've had something good—no, something *great*. Maybe we still could.

"Oh, just work," I replied. "Same old thing with a little added on since Ms. Rosa is out of town right now. Thankfully, she'll be back tomorrow."

He nodded. "Rochelle, I really want to thank you for being willing to give us another chance. I've never been able to forgive myself for Starla's behavior. I'm glad you were finally able to get past it."

I leaned back in my chair and sighed. "I *am* past it, but I hope she won't be a problem for us in the future."

He smiled. "I like the sound of the words 'us' and 'future.'"

I blushed a little. I hadn't blushed in years. Maybe the Room Ten thing was working.

"No, she definitely won't be a problem. There's a restraining order, and from what I hear, she has a new object for her obsession. I am so thankful I never had children with her or I'd be tied to her forever."

"Do you want kids, Vance? I mean, you're so good with them."

"I'd love to have children, but the clock is ticking. I'm not getting any younger and I like women my own age, mature women. I'm not opposed to having stepchildren."

"Really? Well, that's good to know."

"Hmm. Well, I'd better head back to work. That twenty-minute drive is waiting for me." He stood from his chair, and I took note of his tall, lean body. Yeah, he was fine, all right.

"Thanks for having lunch with me, Vance. I enjoyed it," I said as I walked him around the house to his car.

He stopped in his tracks, leaned over, and kissed my cheek. "The pleasure was all mine. Dinner tomorrow night?"

"I don't know. It'll be my first night back at home in a while. How about I call you later and we can make arrangements for another evening?"

"Sounds great."

***

I was actually afraid to go to sleep that night. I'd had such a good day, from my lunch with Vance, to a conflict-free conversation over the phone with Justin. He loved spending time with my folks, and I was glad they had lifted his usually sour mood. I missed him and hoped his mood would remain the same when we both returned home the next day.

So after having a lovely dinner with Dee Dee and our repeat guests, who drove all the way from South Carolina for a little R and R at Hyacinth Manor, I was in good mood, hopeful about the future, and had no desire to take a trip back into the past to revisit my mistakes and regrets.

I lay awake until well past midnight when my eyelids became so heavy I had no choice but to let them fall, and as suspected, *he* invaded my dreams once again.

We were on a Caribbean island because he woke up that morning and decided he wanted to take the trip. Told me to pack and be ready by noon. I gladly obliged, though I hadn't been feeling well for a week or so. I was hoping the change of scenery and weather would do me good. We'd been staying in New York while he finished up some work, and it had snowed nearly every day we were there. Having grown up in Arkansas, where most winters were mild and brought little snow, I wasn't a fan of New York's weather. I also didn't like the people who hung around him there. They all seemed to be pulling at him, trying to get something from him—old friends from the earlier years of his career who felt he owed them something. They always had somewhere they wanted to take him or something they wanted to show him, and well, they were monopolizing his time, taking him away from me, and I didn't like it at all. I wanted my man back, and was glad to know he would be all mine in the Caribbean.

He rented a bungalow, and we spent two weeks doing what we did best when we were together—making love, getting high, getting drunk, eating good food, laughing at nothing, and enjoying each other as if neither of us had a care in the world, and at that point, we didn't. We just had each other.

"I wish it could always be like this," I voiced as we lay naked, side by side, on a blanket on a private beach.

"It will be one day."

"Really?"

"Yeah."

I turned to face him, raised up on one elbow. "You still high or something?"

His brown eyes sparkled as he chuckled and shook his head. "No. Not high at all."

"You have to work. How could we ever live like this permanently?"

"I'm not gonna work forever, Chelly. Shoot, I can't. Who could keep this up forever? I want to settle down, get married, have kids, and you're the only woman I can see myself doing any of that with."

"How long I gotta wait?"

"Not long, Chelly. Not long."

"Hmmm."

"Hey, what do you wanna do? Like, what's your dream, baby?"

I lay back and stared up at the clear sky. "I used to have a lot of dreams but none of them came true, because I could never really focus on one thing. I guess I just want to be somebody, you know? I want to be more than the girl from the hick town."

"You wanna be a star?"

I nodded. "I guess so."

He rolled over until he was on top of me and smiled down at me. "Baby, you are definitely a star."

"You talking about sex?"

He chuckled. "Well, that's a part of it, but that's not all. You're beautiful and fine and kind and everything I need you to be. You're good to me and for me. I love you, baby."

I raised my head and kissed him. "I love you, too."

A week later, I found out I was pregnant.

This time I woke up crying. I hated crying; it always made my head hurt and my face puffy. I hated myself for remembering that day. I hated that I kept thinking about a man who probably hadn't given me a second thought in years.

7

"Family Affair"

I was so glad to see Ms. Rosa back, I didn't know what to do! I loved her like a play mama, even though she was only twelve years older than me, and I had missed her. She was glowing, wearing a bright blue pant suit, her gorgeous gray afro freshly shaped up. She smiled at me when she entered my office, and I stood and hugged her tightly. She had been a rock in my life for a long time. I'd known her nearly all my life, and she was a great help to me when I returned home with a swollen belly and a broken heart. She gave me a job and even let me live in the manor for a while so I wouldn't have to add insult to injury by moving back home with my folks. I was eventually able to buy a house of my own with the generous amount of child support I received from my sperm donor.

That was one of the reasons I was so serious about my job, although it wasn't the best paying job. Ms. Dorcas, Dee Dee, and I were all loyal employees because of our love and appreciation for Ms. Rosa, whose heart was as big as the contiguous United States. She'd been kind and generous to all of us in different ways.

After our hug, she looked at me and frowned slightly. She walked over to my door, closed it, and took a seat across from my desk. "What's wrong, sugar?" she asked gently.

"Nothing," I lied as I reclaimed my seat. "Tell me about your trip.

How was your son?"

"No, ma'am, you're not going to sit there and lie to my face like I don't know you, Rochelle Warrior, like I don't know your mama and daddy and all your aunties, uncles, and cousins. What's wrong? You've been crying. I can tell."

My eyes clouded almost instantly. Ms. Rosa had been my confidant for years, and I'd missed talking to her while she was gone. I just didn't want to burden her as soon as she walked through the door. I shared that concern with her.

"Sugar, we are as close as we can get to family. I'm not some fair-weather friend. Tell me what's wrong."

I told her about Justin's mouth and my decision to try dating Vance again. I was too embarrassed to tell her I'd been dreaming about Justin's father.

She looked at me for a second. "What else?"

I knew better than to try to keep anything from her. She could see through just about anyone. Yet, I still lied. "Nothing."

She sat there with her hands folded in her lap and gave me an expectant look.

I sighed. "I've been having some strange dreams. Memories, really."

"About…"

"Justin's father."

She shifted in her chair. "Hmm, well… I'm not surprised. You've never dealt with that pain. Not really."

"I don't want to deal with it."

"Well, it sounds and looks like it wants to deal with you."

I dropped my eyes.

"You think going out with Vance will fix things, take your mind off the past?"

"I hope so."

"Hmm, well, let me know how that works out for you." She stood and moved toward the door.

"What is that supposed to mean?"

"It means what it means."

There she goes with that cryptic crap. "Wait, that's it? No words of wisdom for me?"

"No, none. Let me go see how Dorcas and Dee Dee are doing."

"But, Rosa—"

She opened the door and stepped into the hall. "I'll talk to you later. Seems like you got a lot to think about."

I released a frustrated sigh as she closed the door behind her.

***

I pulled up to my parents' house, started to blow the horn for Justin to come out, and then thought better of it. I hadn't actually stepped foot in their house in weeks. If I didn't go in there and at least show my face, I was in for a mother of a blessing out.

I stepped in through the unlocked screen door and headed to the kitchen where I knew my daddy was busy with his favorite pastime—cooking. For as long as I could remember, he'd done the cooking, even when my mother stopped working to stay at home and take care of my younger cousins, Saba and Nala—daughters of my father's sister, Maggie—who they ended up raising to adulthood. Now those two didn't even bother to visit my folks. I was their only biological child.

"Hey, Daddy," I greeted as I walked up behind him and tapped his shoulder.

He turned from the sizzling skillet of fried chicken and pulled me into a bear hug. At seventy, Daddy was still tall and wide and as handsome as he was as a young man, despite his balding hair which was dotted with patches of gray. "Hey, puddin'! You come to pick up the boy?"

I smiled at the nickname he'd given Justin almost from the moment he was born.

"Yeah, and I see you're cooking up some of your famous chicken."

He nodded as he turned back to his work. "Yep, used all sixteen of the Warrior secret recipe herbs and spices."

I took a seat at the kitchen table. "You still not gonna give me the recipe, Daddy?"

"No, ma'am. Not until you learn to cook chicken. Hell, not until you learn to cook *period*."

So, me and Justin basically lived on a diet of take-out and fast food—but he didn't have to rub it in. "Really, Daddy? Well, maybe if you share the family recipe with me, it'll motivate me to cook better."

"Humph, if them cooking classes you took out in California that I paid for didn't help, I don't see how this recipe will. Southern women are supposed to automatically be good cooks."

"Mama can't cook, either," I countered.

"Lord, don't I know it," he mumbled.

I giggled and tried to stop when Mama entered the red and white Coca Cola-themed kitchen. "What you in here sniggling about, girl?" she asked as her eyes landed on Daddy's back. "You better not be talking about me, Nate."

I gave my mother, whose youthful genes I'd inherited, a sheepish expression. Standing there in jeans and a t-shirt, my sixty-eight-year-old mother could've easily passed for a woman in her forties.

"Ain't nobody talking about you, woman. Always trying to start something. I was just in here talking to my daughter."

My parents had been fighting like cats and dogs for as long as I could remember, which was probably why they didn't get married until I was eight years old. But they loved each other. That much I was sure of.

"She's my daughter, too, Negro."

"Hell, I know that, Martha. Why you gotta come in here and break my peace?"

"Ain't nobody tryna break your peace. When the damn chicken gon' be done, anyway?"

"In about ten minutes. You want yours extra crispy, baby?"

"You know I do."

"All right. Come give me some sugar."

She walked over to him and quickly obliged.

I just shook my head at them.

Mama took a seat across from me. "I got Justin out back raking leaves."

I nodded. "It's nice he'll do that for you. I can't get him to sweep the kitchen, let alone do labor outside."

She glanced up at my father who must've had eyes in his back, because he took the cue and said, "Let me go see how the boy is doing out there. Martha, don't let my chicken burn."

"I won't," Mama said, and then she turned her attention to me. "We need to talk about Justin."

I sighed, wished I'd just honked the horn. "Yes, ma'am?"

"Now, your daddy and I love spending time with him, and he's always welcome here, but you need to spend more time with that boy."

"Mama, I spend plenty of time with him. Did he say I don't?"

"He doesn't have to say it, baby. His actions tell the story. The boy needs more attention from you. You're always at work, barely have dinner with him. You need to spend more time getting to know your son."

"Getting to know—okay, okay…look, Mama, I have to work, and work requires me to stay past dinnertime every once in a while."

"All that money you got in the bank, those big checks his daddy keeps sending, and you *have* to work?"

"That money is Justin's, not mine. He said that himself the other day."

"You can't let that drop, huh?"

"I only brought it up because we were talking about money. Anyway, I don't want to depend on that money. I don't want to have to scramble to find a job when Justin turns eighteen. And besides, I love my job. Is there a crime against that?"

"Only if you use that job to dodge your parenting responsibilities."

"I think you have the wrong parent in mind. His father is the only major league dodger in his life."

"You're a close second."

With a furrowed brow, I said, "Wow, okay. You know what? I won't bother you with my son anymore. I will take care of him all by myself from now on. Don't worry about me bothering you or burdening you with taking care of him. I got him, like I always have. I had him alone and I'll raise him alone." I snatched my keys up from the Coca Cola polar bear place matt and quickly stood to my feet. I wasn't about to sit there and let my mother insult my parenting and put me in the same category with *him*. I loved and respected her, but she had crossed the line for sure.

She placed a hand on my arm. I looked down at her to see concern in her smooth, dark brown face. "Wait. Now you know that's not what I meant. I know you do the best you can, and maybe you're just tired because you're an older mother, way older than I was when I raised you, but I don't think you're seeing things clearly. You're a good mother, Rochelle, *you are*. And I know you love that boy more than anything in the world. All I'm saying—and I'm saying it with the love of a concerned mother and grandmother—is that this is a crucial time in his life. He's becoming a man and needs a father to teach him things. Now, your daddy tries to teach him what he can, but it's not the same. Just try to give him a little more attention, okay?"

I twisted my mouth. She had hit a nerve that gentle words couldn't easily repair. "I gotta go."

"I know you're mad at me, but y'all might as well stay for dinner. You know you want some of your daddy's chicken, and you know you ain't about to go home and cook."

I fumbled with my keys. "We were gonna have dinner at the manor."

"Old Dorcas can cook, but she ain't got nothing on Nate's chicken and you know it."

You ain't never lied. I reclaimed my seat. "Yeah, I guess we can stay."

Dinner was actually pleasant, and Justin looked relieved to see me. I was glad to see him, too, and glad to be taking him home. After we both got settled back in, I called Rosa and told her I wouldn't be able to stay late any more for a while. She understood my need to spend more time with Justin. As much as I hated to admit it, Mama was right. I was tired, and in my own way, I had been running away from my responsibilities. I was going to work to correct that.

The next morning, Justin and I ate our bowls of cereal together at the dining room table in my modest home. I stole several glances at him, marveled at how much he'd changed in the few days he'd spent with my folks. He seemed to be growing taller by the second, his thick hair needed to be cut again, and as he looked up at me with his father's eyes, I felt my heart twist a little.

"What?" he asked.

I shook my head. "Nothing—you ready to get back to school?"

"Yeah."

"Yeah?"

"Yes, ma'am," he mumbled.

"Don't forget to apologize to Ms. Kendall."

"I know. I won't forget."

He finished his cereal, tossed his bowl into the sink, and was poised to leave the room when I said, "I love you, and I know we haven't spent enough time together lately. I'm going to do better, spend less time at work."

He looked a little surprised. "Okay."

"I love you, Justin. More than anything."

"I love you, too, Ma."

8

"Lately"

*"**I** wanna tell you something, Chelly."*

I was seated next to him on the sofa in the little room. Musty smoke filled the air. He squinted as he looked at me and handed me the joint. I shook my head in refusal since I was pregnant, though I hadn't mustered up the nerve to tell him. He shrugged, took another toke, and slowly exhaled smoke.

"What is it?" I asked.

"I had a messed up life before all of this success, Chelly. My mama was strung out on drugs, eventually OD'd. I don't even know who my daddy is. Grew up in foster homes, saw some jacked up stuff, went through some jacked up stuff. Hell, if I don't stay high, I can't sleep at night."

"I... I'm sorry."

"What about you? How was your childhood, baby?"

"My parents weren't perfect, but they took care of me the best they could. They still do."

"They still help you, grown as you are?"

I smiled. "It's crazy, right? They're good people, though. Always got my back."

"Sounds like it. You know, I'll never understand how a man can make kids and then abandon them like my father did me. Never

wonder about them, if they're okay or got enough to eat. Hell, I'd never do my kids like that. I'ma be there for them and their mama."

I smiled. It was such a relief to hear that.

I woke up that morning and decided to ignore that dream. He'd obviously lied back then, so I wasn't about to waste time, energy, or tears on that memory.

I spent the next couple of months being a better mother to my son, listening to him, reminiscing with him, laughing with him, and it was great. We had a wonderful Thanksgiving and Christmas; both of which Vance celebrated with us at my parents' house. Vance and I were seeing each other regularly, and things were going well between us. I wasn't in love with him yet, but I really felt like those sparks were just around the corner. So when he offered to take me to a Stevie Wonder concert in Little Rock, I jumped at the chance and hesitantly left Justin with my parents who seemed happy to have him back after a long hiatus save our holiday gatherings. It was a plus that my folks liked Vance. But I honestly think they were just happy to see me spending time with a man. I wasn't getting any younger, and my mama had been wishing for a wedding for me for a years, long before Justin came along.

We had dinner at Genghis Grill first, enjoyed some good conversation as we ate some good food. And when it was time to head to the concert arena, I was full and content and ready for the legendary music master to dazzle me.

Vance had to park a couple of blocks away, so we had to take a little trek to the arena. I loved the way he held my hand. I loved the way his jeans and sweater fit him. I loved the way his cologne rode the light breeze and settled in my nose. I loved his smile and his laugh. But most of all, I loved how patient he'd been with me those couple of months as I tried to strengthen my bond with my son. And I loved how he interacted with Justin. I had a feeling that Room Ten was working its magic on me, and maybe, just maybe, I'd love him, too, by the end of the night.

Once we made it inside and arrived at the excellent seats Vance bought for us—fifth row, center—I took in our surroundings, smiled as excitement began to build inside of me. It had been a long time since I'd been to a concert or anywhere fun, for that matter. Seeing the stage and the tons of people piling into the arena really thrilled me.

We settled into our seats, and Vance wrapped his long arm around my shoulders. "You ready for Stevie?" he asked.

"Yes! Thanks so much for this, Vance. I can't tell you how long it's been since I've done something like this."

He leaned in and whispered, "Stick with me, and you'll being doing stuff like this all the time. I'll do nothing but spoil you."

My skin tingled where his warm breath caressed it. I smiled and thought to myself: *Go, Room Ten!*

Stevie Wonder—what can I say? Being in that place, listening to a musical legend, and seeing him live and in person was nothing short of monumental. So many good songs connected to good memories. So much talent in one human being. It was actually kind of overwhelming to hear and watch him go through his repertoire, but I was so glad to be there and glad to be with Vance.

As the night wore on, I grew tired since I wasn't used to being out that late, but I was determined to enjoy myself. So I stood and danced during the upbeat songs. Vance stood next to me, a grin on his face as he bounced in front of his seat.

During "Isn't She Lovely", Vance sang along with Stevie, tone-deafly serenading me with tenderness in his eyes. When the song was over, he leaned in and gently kissed my lips.

It couldn't have been a better night. As a matter of fact, I was poised to mark it down as one of the best days of my life, until...

Stevie sang "Lately", and it felt like a ton of bricks hit me square in the chest. I should've realized he would sing it. I should've prepared myself. I should've been ready.

But I wasn't.

I fell back into my seat as soon as he began to sing the lyrics. "Lately" was *his* favorite song, but it was Jodeci's version that he'd put on repeat and blast often. He'd sing along or slow dance with me. That song catapulted me into the past so quickly that I actually felt a little light-headed. I was so overwhelmed that during the second verse, I left my seat without even telling Vance where I was going, headed to the concession stand, and returned with a cup of beer.

And I don't even like beer.

I guzzled it down, and though I didn't enjoy it one bit, I soon found myself making my way back to the concession stand for another one. In total, I had five cups of beer before the concert's end. The walk back to the car was so unsteady, I had to lean against it and catch my breath before climbing inside.

"Did you enjoy yourself?" Vance asked as I settled into my seat and he started the car.

"Eeeeyepppp!" I giggled.

"I didn't know you liked beer so much."

"Neither did I." I hiccupped and let out a long burp.

He smiled. "Seatbelt, please. You're precious cargo."

I fumbled with the seatbelt before letting it flop back in its place and blowing out a frustrated sigh.

"Let me help."

As he leaned across me to grab the seatbelt, I kissed his neck. He stopped and stared at me, and I took the opportunity to kiss his lips. A millisecond later, he was kissing me back, wrapping his long arms around me.

When we finally parted, I said, "Justin is spending the night with my folks. Let's get a room."

He stared at my lips. "Okay."

***

I threw up on him.

Inside the nice hotel room, I threw up all over Vance's starched jeans, and then I cried, and then I began to ramble. And then I crawled into the bed and passed out.

The next morning, I was the picture of embarrassment. I rose from the bed, glimpsed at Vance asleep on the floor, and wished I could evaporate into thin air. I wasn't sure which embarrassed me more, the fact that my fifty-year-old tail got drunk, or the fact that I almost had a one-night stand, or the fact that a stupid song had been the catalyst for all of that.

I had been enjoying a great night with a great man and *he* still managed to creep in and ruin everything. I hated him in a new and special way at that moment.

I closed my eyes and slumped back onto the bed, wondering what I had to do to rid my mind of this man. There had to be a way to put the past in the past and leave it there. But how could I do that when I had a fifteen-year-old walking and talking reminder living in my house? How could I love my son so much and hate his father with the same intensity?

"You feeling better?" Vance asked, startling me. I didn't realize he was awake.

"Yes—I'm so, so sorry."

"It's okay."

Awkward silence.

"Whose song was it?" he asked, out of the blue.

"What?" My heart was thudding in my chest. What in the world had I said to him when I was drunk? What did he know?

"You said it was *his* song."

"Oh, no.... W-What else did I say?"

"That you used to make love to it and that he loved that song."

"Oh, Lord..."

"Which song and who is *he*?"

I sat up in the bed. "I really don't want to talk about it. Let's just—can you take me home?"

"Sure, but it's a long ride back to Hyacinth Valley so you may as well tell me now so I won't have to ask again later."

I stood from the bed, walked to the bathroom, and mumbled, "Justin's father. He loved 'Lately'."

9

"Prior to You"

Neither of us had much to say on the way back home. I glanced at him and was thankful he kept a spare set of clothes in his trunk. I wanted to apologize again, but decided to let it drop. Instead, I thought about the song and its lyrics. "Lately" was actually a rather sad song about a man who suspects his woman of cheating and is afraid of losing her. How twisted was it that we made love to it time and time again? Shows you just how messed up we were together.

After an hour of silence, with the exception of the music pouring from Vance's car speakers, he cleared his throat, and said, "I'm sorry if you felt like I was intruding by asking you about what you said last night. I was just curious."

I shook my head and fixed my eyes on the pine trees lining the highway. "No, it's my fault. I can't really hold liquor anymore. There was a time when I could, but that was long ago. So I shouldn't have drunk so much, and then maybe I wouldn't have had that little confessional in your presence."

"You still love him? Justin's father?"

I frowned. "No, on the contrary, I despise him."

"If you dislike him that strongly, you must've really loved him at some point. I've found that only love can bring about that much hate."

I didn't like where the conversation was going. "Well, I can tell you that what I feel for him right now is far from love. Best believe that."

"I believe it."

After a minute or two of silence, he asked, "Does he ever see Justin?"

I shook my head no, silently wishing he would drop the subject of my ex.

"That's a shame. Justin is a great kid."

"I know."

"Rochelle, can I tell you something?"

I nodded yes.

"I'm in love with you, have been since we were together before, and I want to thank you for giving us another chance."

I glanced over at him, unsure of how to feel about his revelation. I wished I could return the sentiment, but it honestly would've been a lie. I didn't love him, yet, but I felt like I could fall in love with him at any moment. "Vance…"

He reached over and grasped one of my hands. "It's okay. You don't have to say it back. I believe your feelings for me will grow in time. I just told you that so you'll understand what my intentions are, that they are the same as they were before. I'm not just trying to date you. I want a future with you. I want to be a father to Justin and a provider, lover, and friend for you."

I squeezed his hand. "I want the same thing."

***

"You're what?" he asked.

His eyes were clear and so was his head, because I'd made sure he wasn't high or drunk before I told him. So I knew he'd heard me, but nevertheless, I repeated myself. "I'm pregnant."

"Pregnant? After all this time? We been doing it for like a year. How? Ain't you on birth control?"

"I was. I don't know how it happened. Maybe I missed a pill when I was high or something one day. But the fact is… I'm pregnant."

He was sitting at the foot of the bed. I was standing against the wall, and my heart was galloping in my chest. He seemed not only shocked, but a little bewildered, like it had never occurred to him that my getting pregnant was a possibility.

"Are you gonna have it?" he asked.

"Well… yeah, I was planning to. I'm not getting any younger, baby, and I want kids, always have. I don't think it would make any sense not to have it."

He shook his head before digging into the front pocket of his hoodie and pulling out a joint. He lit it, took a drag, and shook his head again. "I ain't ready for this."

"Well, I'm not, either, but I guess we need to get ready, because it's happening."

"You can't have it."

My eyes widened. "I can't have it? What do you mean?"

"We should wait, have one later. Not now. I'm not ready."

"Then get ready, like I said."

"If you have that baby, we're over, Chelly. I mean it."

My mouth dropped open. "After all that talk about what a good father you'd be if you had kids and how you'd never abandon your kids, this is what you have to say?"

"Just because I told you that didn't mean you had to try to trap me!" he shouted as he stood from the bed and invaded my personal space.

"Trap you! Really? That's what you think of me? I thought you loved me like I love you."

"I do love you. That's why it hurts to know you'd do this to me. I trusted you! Is it about the money, Chelly? I would've given you the world, but now I don't want nothing to do with you."

He stormed out of the room, a hotel room he'd rented for a short stay in Miami while he completed some work. He never came back to that hotel room, and the next time I saw him was a little over a year later in court, where I sued him for child support.

This time, the memories came to me as I sat in the passenger seat of Vance's car. I was wide awake, but helpless to stop the flood of images that filled my mind. When he pulled into my driveway, I thanked him, promised to see him at church that Sunday, and then went into my house and cried.

10

"Love Under New Management"

Ms. Dorcas's birthday was always a big event at Hyacinth Manor, and it was made even more special after she became a breast cancer survivor three years earlier. Ms. Rosa and I worked hard to prepare for the celebration. The party itself was never a surprise, but we made sure to keep the theme and any special guests a secret from her.

Her birthday party was the one manor occasion when she was not expected to cook, as Ms. Rosa always hired a caterer. Dee Dee did the bulk of the decorating with my assistance, and I made most of the other arrangements. I loved preparing for this annual event. I especially enjoyed helping to prepare for the special surprises that were in store for her this time.

Two weeks had passed since the fateful concert date, but Vance and I were still going strong with lunch dates and Sunday dinners at his house. He was a great cook and a wonderful conversationalist and he loved me—I truly believed and felt that from him. He was the perfect package, and I grew fonder and fonder of him with each passing day. I saw a good future for us, and for the first time in my life, I was truly ready to become a Mrs.

As I sat at my desk the day of the party, I was content, happy with the direction my life was headed in, and thankful that the onslaught of dreams and memories had stopped. *He* was no longer intruding on my life and stealing away my happiness. He'd done enough of that to last a lifetime.

"Penny for your thoughts?"

Ms. Rosa's voice pulled me back to the present. I looked up and gave her a smile. "Hey. I didn't hear you come in here."

"I know, because from the looks of it, you had something heavy on your mind."

I shrugged. "Just thoughts. Can I help you with something?"

She eyed me as she took a seat in front of my desk. "Just wanted to make sure everything's set for tonight."

I nodded. "I was just looking over everything, and yes, I think we're ready. I love this year's theme. I think Ms. Dorcas is gonna love it, too."

"Good. Speaking of love, how are things with you and Vance? I noticed you two sit together every Sunday at church now."

I gave her a grin. "Going great. He's such a good man. I'm glad I gave things a second chance."

"Hmm," she said, her eyes on me.

Here we go. "What is that supposed to mean? You don't think Vance is a good man?"

She held up a hand. "Oh, no, not that. Vance is a great person, one of the sweetest, kindest men I've ever known. Loves kids, has a good job and a nice house…"

"What's the *but*? I can tell there's a *but*."

"But… I just never saw him as your type."

"Really, and who *did* you see as my type?"

"Lord, there you go with that attitude of yours."

"I don't have an attitude."

"Then why are you rolling your neck with every word you say?"

"I'm not," I denied, but I probably was. I had a bad habit of doing that when I was irritated or annoyed.

"You just rolled your eyes."

I sighed and folded my arms over my chest.

"Your type is definitely *not* Vance Washington. If he was your type, you two never would've broken up in the first place."

"You know why we broke up. I wasn't feeling the whole psycho ex thing."

"But that was her, not him. Everyone knows Starla Littleton is crazy. You knew it when you started dating him. Her actions were just an excuse you used to get out of a relationship you didn't want to be in in the first place."

"So now you're a mind reader?"

"No, but I have the gift of discernment. You know that."

"And you discern what? That I didn't like him?"

"Mm-hmm, and that you *still* don't, not really. He loves you. Ray Charles could see that. But you definitely don't love him. Vance is a placeholder."

I leaned forward with a deep frown on my face. This woman was insane! "A placeholder? A placeholder for who?"

"For the man you really love."

"And who might that be, Rosa?"

"You know better than I do." And of course she left without allowing me to ask her what the hell she meant, because she specialized in cryptic speech and she knew that crap got under my skin.

***

The theme for the Ms. Dorcas's party was, "Hop aboard the Soul Train." The main hall was decorated with mirror balls hanging from the high ceiling and psychedelic artwork adorning the walls. Strobe lights flashed in time with the beat of seventies soul jams. There was a dancefloor with enough room to cut a good rug, surrounded by round tables covered with tie-dyed tablecloths. Seventies fashion was every guest's admission fee, and bell bottoms and afros abounded. This year, like every other year, we bought Ms. Dorcas's outfit for the party. So while Dee Dee was upstairs helping her change into her "flower power" dress and afro wig, I made the rounds in my form-sitting leisure jumpsuit. I had placed beads on the ends of my signature box braids and was carefully trying to balance myself in my platform shoes. Vance looked so handsome in his bell bottom jeans and dashiki top. I couldn't wait to hit the dancefloor with him and show those folks what I could do.

The buffet line was filling up as folks loaded their plates with finger foods and my daddy's famous fried chicken, which he'd graciously cooked and donated to the affair. I was happy with the turnout, and when Ms. Dorcas finally made her entrance, I was proud to see the grin on her face. Soul Train had always been her favorite show. She still had VHS tapes of it that she watched from time to time, but as delighted as she was, she had no idea just what was in store for her.

Satisfied that everything was running smoothly, I finally settled at the table I shared with my decked-out and color-coordinated parents, Justin, and Vance. We talked and observed the enthusiastic party-goers. Ms. Rosa could be seen on the dancefloor dancing with Greg, the groundskeeper she'd recently hired to replace the newlywed August Donovan, who had moved overseas with his wife months earlier. She looked radiant in a red jumpsuit and her bare feet with red toenails. Her afro was shaped up to perfection. At sixty-two, she always made heads turn. It wasn't that she didn't look her age, it was how she wore it. She was proud of it and carried herself with a sense of elegance. I wanted to be just like her when I reached that age.

I nearly died when I spotted Ms. Dorcas's seventy-seven-year-old boyfriend, Farris, on the dancefloor, stiffly dancing to the DJ's mashup of Sister Sledge's "He's the Greatest Dancer" with Chic's "Dance, Dance, Dance". His jerky arm movements were so comical, I eventually had to rush to the bathroom before I peed on myself.

Then it was time for the big surprise. Farris took to the small, empty stage at the end of the room, pulled the microphone from its stand, and asked that everyone take a seat at their tables. A hush grew over the room as everyone settled down and gave him their attention.

"I wanna thank all of y'all for coming out tonight and helping to celebrate my Dorcas's birthday. She turned seventy-one today. Here's to another seventy-one years, baby!"

Everyone cheered and raised their glasses to salute Ms. Dorcas, who stood from her seat with a huge grin on her face and gave us a little curtsy.

"Now, I know my lady's heart, so I want to announce that my gift to her is a $10,000 donation to the Susan Komen Foundation."

Applause erupted along with a chorus of "wows." But everyone knew the wealthy Farris Kenwood was a generous man.

"Now, for the real surprise," he teased, then left the stage.

Those who didn't know what was about to happen whispered to one another and wore curious and confused expressions. I just smiled.

When a small band began to set up, the buzz in the room grew louder.

When the one and only, Smokey Robinson, stepped onto the stage, the buzz grew into an excited roar.

The applause was so loud, you could barely hear Smokey as he thanked everyone. It took several minutes for the surprised attendees to settle down, and my heart swelled when I saw Ms. Dorcas grab Farris and kiss him full on the lips. Smokey Robinson was her favorite singer—anyone who knew her knew that—and Farris had truly made this a special birthday for her by arranging for him to perform.

Mr. Robinson's falsetto voice was so clear, hearing and seeing him perform was like listening to a greatest hits CD. I swayed to the music in my chair as the dancefloor began to fill up again. When he sang "Being with You", Vance reached for my hand and led me to the floor where I rested my head against his broad chest and closed my eyes. The night and that moment felt so… magical. It was then that I realized I more than cared for Vance, I was falling for him. So when he released me and fell onto one knee right there on the dancefloor, my heart leaped.

After taking a deep breath, Vance smiled and said, "Rochelle Warrior, will you marry me?"

I gave him a swift "yes" and jumped into his arms once he stood to his feet again. Everyone around us cheered and applauded, including Justin and my parents who were smiling brightly. Well, everyone except for Ms. Rosa. I spotted her disapproving face among the crowd of people. But I didn't care how she felt about it. This was my opportunity for real happiness, and I was seizing it. I was going to marry this tall, fine man, and after a fifteen-year drought, I was going to spend my honeymoon getting my groove back!

"Congratulations!" Farris shouted into the microphone. He was standing next to Smokey on the stage. "But I think you upstaged me a bit. You see," he paused as he slowly made his way from the stage to the table he shared with Ms. Dorcas and her hulking sons. "I had the same thing in mind." The older man knelt before where Ms. Dorcas sat in her chair. "Dorcas May Malone, will you marry me?"

"Yessssss!" she screamed, eliciting more applause.

I rushed over to the couple, joined by Dee Dee and Rosa, and hugged both Ms. Dorcas and Farris. "Y'all knew this was gon' happen, didn't you?" she asked though tears. "Y'all lowdown for keeping this from me."

"We couldn't spoil your surprise," I said. "Let me see that ring, Ms. Dorcas."

"Only if you let me see yours," she replied.

I grinned and pulled her into another hug. It was a wonderful night for both of us.

11

"What Am I Gonna Do"

"I wanna meet my father."

I sat there at the table with a bowl of Raisin Bran in front of me and darn near dropped my spoon. It was Saturday, the one day I never did anything if I didn't have to work. Shoot, I even kept my pajamas on all day most Saturdays, but Justin's announcement had put a serious damper on the start of my day and had shocked me. "What?" I finally managed to say.

"I wanna meet my father. I have for a long time."

"W-why? I mean—why?"

He shrugged. "He's half of me. I wanna meet him in person, see how he really is."

"Um… Justin, he—I don't know if that's a good idea. I don't want you to get hurt."

"I know he doesn't really want anything to do with me. I mean, I don't think we'll be buddies or anything like that. I just wanna meet him so he can see me and I can see him. That's all."

"Um… I see."

"Can you get in touch with him?"

"Now?" My appetite was gone. My mouth was dry. I wanted nothing more than to crawl back into bed.

"Can you?"

"Um... let me see what I can do, but it's not that easy to get in touch with him. He's a busy man, Justin."

"I know, but please try. *Please*."

I sighed and pushed my cereal away. Justin had been nothing but respectful for months, and we'd been getting along well. His grades were good, no more calls from the school. Things were so peaceful, and I was in a really good place... and now *this*.

"Ma, will you? I know you hate him, so I was kinda scared to ask you before, but will you please do it?"

"I don't hate—" I cut my own lie off, and I felt kind of bad that he knew I felt that way. I really needed to watch what I said around him, but I suppose it was already too late for that.

"Ma?"

Lord, help me. "Okay... okay."

***

I held the crumpled letter, which I had fished out of the trash months ago, in my hand and stared at it. Like I said before, Justin's father had taken to writing letters to him for the last five years or so, but he always addressed them to me. I'd never shown them to Justin. I never even told him about them, but I always read them and then threw them away since I knew his words were just empty promises he'd never fulfill, because he was incapable of fulfilling them. But I'd found it impossible to even open this most recent letter, and I'd found it equally as impossible to leave it in the trash, so I'd stashed it in one of my drawers until this day. Without opening it, I knew what it would say—that he was sorry for the past but that he wanted to have a chance at being a father to Justin. And as always, the letter would end with his phone number and email address. It had been months since I received it, and I told myself that the information might not have even been valid anymore. Then I remembered the look in my boy's eyes when he made the request, and I tore the envelope open. I had to try… for him.

I closed my eyes, took a deep breath, and began to read the words written in his scrawled handwriting:

Dear Chelly,

I hope you and Justin are doing well.

I think about both of you two all the time. I want to again apologize for my actions in the past. I know you're probably still angry at me and I don't blame you. What I did was despicable and I am ashamed of myself. I still hope you will one day forgive me. But even if you don't, I hope you'll find it in your heart to let me see our son. I love him, Chelly, and I want more than anything to be a part of his life.

If you decide to let me see him, you can reach me via phone or email. My contact information is at the bottom of this letter.

Yours Truly,

T

I grabbed my phone from the bedside table, prayed for strength,

and then dialed his number.

12

"Real Life"

"You called him? You talked to him?"

I knew this was a mistake. Instead of asking Ms. Rosa to reserve a room for him, I should've just booked him a room in one of the larger towns nearby. "Yes and yes."

"Really? You didn't cuss him out? How'd he sound?"

"No, I didn't cuss him out and he sounded like... himself." I shuddered a little at the memory of hearing his voice again after so many years.

"What'd you say to him?"

I was standing by her desk because I thought this would be a quick conversation, but Rosa knew my history, so of course she'd want to hear every detail. I took a seat in her office and crossed my legs. "He said hello, I told him who I was, he said he was glad I called."

"He did?"

"Yes. And he apologized for the things that happened in the past and said he hoped we could eventually be friends."

She leaned forward. "What'd you say?"

"I said I already have friends and I'm not looking to make any new ones."

"Lord, sugar..."

"He said he understood and asked what made me call."

"And..."

"I told him Justin wants to meet him."

She raised her eyebrows.

"And he got all excited like this is a dream come true for him or something."

"Maybe it is."

"Mm-hmm, anyhow, then he said he'd be here in a few days—on Friday. So can you reserve him a room and please be discreet?"

She reclined in her seat. "Now, Rochelle Warrior, I'm insulted. You think I'd tell someone?"

"No, I know you better than that. I'm talking about Dee Dee. You know how nosy she is when it comes to the guests."

"That's true. But girl, she's still riding high from meeting her cousin Smokey and getting his autograph. That's all she talks about."

I chuckled. "How many cousins does Dee Dee have?"

"Let her tell it, she's related to half of the Motown roster. Well, I'm glad Justin's going to meet his dad."

"Me, too. I just hope he doesn't get disappointed."

"Sugar, the only thing we can do about that is pray."

I nodded, knowing that was exactly what I was going to do.

"What made you decide to call him for Justin anyway?"

"The look in my son's eyes. He's desperate to meet him. Plus, he's been acting like he has sense and we've been getting along and I didn't want to risk messing that up, so I couldn't refuse."

"I'm glad you didn't."

13

"Hey Daddy"

I was nervous the entire day. I couldn't concentrate, I had no appetite, and my hands wouldn't stop shaking. A lot of years had passed, and although I wanted Justin to be happy, I wished more than anything for his father to call and cancel, or just fail to show up, or *something*. I didn't want to see him. Talking to him on the phone was hard enough, but seeing him in the flesh? I just wasn't sure if I could survive that.

A blood-curdling scream snatched me from my thoughts and sent me to my feet. I recognized the voice as being Dee Dee's, and since we had no guests at the moment, I wondered if one of my coworkers had passed out or something. After all, none of us were spring chickens.

I rushed into the foyer to find her standing in the open front doorway, screaming at the top of her lungs. Ms. Dorcas and Ms. Rosa appeared in the foyer, too. "Dee Dee, what is it?!" Ms. Rosa asked.

"It's Teo B! Teo B is here!! Right there! Look!" She pointed outside.

My stomach dropped.

Ms. Rosa gave me a knowing look.

Ms. Dorcas said, "Who?"

Dee Dee turned around with shock in her eyes. "*Who?!* Teo B! That man can sing and dance like nobody else and he's so fine it don't make no sense. He's a superstar, Ms. Dorcas!"

"He's famous? Are you sure that's him? What's he doing here?" Ms. Dorcas asked.

"He's Justin's dad," I murmured.

"What?! You know Teo B, got a baby by him, and you never told me?" Dee Dee shrieked.

"It wasn't something I wanted to talk about and please don't tell anyone he's here, Dee Dee."

"She won't unless she wants to deal with me," Ms. Rosa said.

Teo, who was standing next to a shiny black car, ascended the front steps wearing white pants, a white dress shirt, and a white fedora. No jacket, though the late January air was biting. He also wore shades, and I wondered if his eyes were bloodshot because the sky was gray and there was no sun out. Was he high? Drunk?

He reached the top step, approached the open door, and removed his shades. His eyes weren't bloodshot. As a matter of fact, they were clear and as beautiful and sad as I remembered them being.

All four of us backed away as he entered the manor. Dee Dee backed into a table.

"Lord, that's a fine man," Ms. Dorcas uttered under her breath.

"Mm-hmm," Ms. Rosa agreed.

He stepped in front of me, gazed down at me. "Chelly."

"Chelly?" I faintly heard Dee Dee say. "I didn't know he was so tall," she added. Then I heard Rosa shush her.

"T-baby—I mean, T," I stammered.

"T-baby? She called him T-baby?" Dee Dee asked.

Ms. Rosa stepped forward and extended her hand. "I'm Rosa, the owner of Hyacinth Manor. It's a pleasure to have you. This is Dorcas, who'll be preparing all of your meals, and—"

"I'm Dee Dee, your number one fan! I love 'Your Body'! Well, I love all of your stuff and I'm really glad to meet you. Can I get an autograph for—"

"Dee Dee is the housekeeper," Ms. Rosa continued. "If you'll excuse us, I'll let Rochelle check you in."

"Thank you, Rosa," he said in a voice that was so familiar, the hairs on my arms stood up.

They left—well, Ms. Rosa *dragged* Dee Dee away. All the while she was yelling something about how much she loved the song he did with Drake. Then there we stood, face to face for the first time in more than a decade. After a few moments, I finally turned and walked to the front desk. He followed me and slid his black card to me. "Thank you for this," he said as I handed his card back to him.

"I'm doing it for Justin, not for you."

"Still, I appreciate it. I really do."

"Mm-hmm. No bodyguards or security?"

"No one knows I'm here. I figured I'd give them some time off."

I nodded. "Well, let me show you to your room. You're in number three."

"Psst! Ask him if he'll let me record him singing a little something on my phone." It was Dee Dee again, but I have no idea how she managed to get away from Ms. Rosa.

"Dee Dee," I began, but Ms. Rosa interrupted me with, "Dee Dee! You better get back in here unless you want to be in the unemployment line in the morning!" She shuffled away and I shook my head.

With a furrowed brow, he asked, "Is she gonna be okay? Am I safe here?"

"She's harmless, just a little strange."

He nodded.

I took a deep breath and led him up the stairs to his room.

"It's beautiful," he said once we arrived.

"Yes, well, you can only take your meals in the dining room. Times are posted in the information pamphlet next to your bed. You have towels in the bathroom, and if you need anything, just let us know. After hours, any calls you make to the front desk will ring directly to Ms. Rosa's room. She lives here."

As I turned to leave, he stopped me in my tracks with, "When can I see our son?"

I cringed at the words, *our son.* "He has basketball practice. I was going to bring him here to meet you after I pick him up."

"Does he know I'm here? Did you tell him I was coming?"

"No. I was afraid you'd back out."

He nodded. "I understand. Um, can I come to his practice?"

I frowned. "Aren't you afraid of being recognized?"

"I'll wear my shades, and besides, I don't think anyone would expect to see me here."

"Those shades didn't stop Dee Dee from recognizing you."

"I'll wear a hat, too."

"You might want to change into something less noticeable, as well."

"Is that a yes?"

I sighed. "Be ready at four."

"Thank you. I will."

My legs felt like they were made of runny gelatin as I descended the stairs and rushed into my office, where I dropped into my chair and laid my head on my desk. He smelled the same, looked the same, sounded the same, and being in his presence was overwhelming. It wasn't like I hadn't seen his face plastered all over the Internet or seen his tons of videos or heard his music on the radio all the time. As a matter of fact, I was numb to those experiences. The difference between seeing or hearing him in those instances and actually being in his presence was akin to the difference between watching a volcano erupt on TV and standing at the bottom of it as it spewed lava. The heat of the volcano that was Mateo Bridges, AKA The Prince of R&B, AKA Billboard's Entertainer of the Year for five years running, AKA award-winning artist, Teo B, was stifling.

"You okay?"

I looked up to see Rosa standing in my doorway. "Hell, no. Are you? Is anybody? You saw him. I can't stand him and *I* wanna ask for an autograph."

"He does have a presence about him, and the TV and Internet do not do him justice. He is one handsome man."

"I know."

Dee Dee burst into the room. "How the hell you gon' keep something like this a secret, *Chelly*?"

"I had to. Look at how you're acting."

"I can't help it! I was caught off guard!"

"Me, too."

Dee Dee plopped her wide behind down on the edge of my desk. "How'd you meet him? What's the skinny?"

"Dee Dee, leave her alone," Rosa said.

I shook my head. "If I don't tell her, she'll probably just ask *him*. This whole thing was just a bad idea." I sighed. "He picked me to be in one of his videos, and I ended up being his girlfriend for more than a year. It was a very intense relationship."

"What?! How come I never saw any pictures of you with him? What video?"

"'Your Body'. I was the girl whose back he dripped honey on."

"That was *your* back? Girl, you have a nice back!"

"It's a much older back now. And there are pictures of us. I was younger, wore shades a lot." *Because I was usually high.*

"I read somewhere that he had a kid, but that kid is *your* kid?" Dee Dee asked. She glanced at the picture of Justin sitting on my desk. "That boy looks like him! How have I never noticed that before?"

I shrugged.

"Teo B ever sing to you when you two were together?"

"All the time."

She hopped up and headed out of my office.

"Where you going?" Rosa asked.

"To find those pictures. I'ma use the Internet on my phone."

"Dee Dee!" both Rosa and I said in unison.

"I'm not gonna tell anyone!" she shouted as she rushed away from us.

"What happened to being discreet?" Rosa asked.

"I had no idea she'd react like that. If I hadn't told her the truth she'd have had no reason not to blab about him being here. It's been so long, I think I forgot what affect he has on people and just how famous he really is. I shoulda just gotten him a room at that motor inn over in Paxton."

"Okay, I know he's not your favorite person, but that motor inn is a crack trap, sugar."

"I know... Can I have a moment?"

"Sure thing. If you need me, you know where I am."

She left and I closed the door behind her and fell on my knees and prayed to God for strength not to kill, or sleep with, *the* Teo B.

***

I made my way to the neighboring town of Paxton, where most children in Hyacinth Valley and other nearby towns with populations too small to sustain their own school districts attended school. The Herbert Rollins High School building was only a couple of years old, having been built to accommodate an ever-growing student population. I graduated from the school years ago when it was housed in a much smaller complex and simply called Paxton High School. I kept my eyes on the road, because I might have veered off of it had I even glanced at the man sitting in my passenger seat. When I went to his room to retrieve him and saw what he was wearing—jeans tailor-made for his body, a fitted black t-shirt, and no shades—my stomach started breakdancing and pop-locking. He was fine, all six-foot-three of him, and every time I looked at him, I saw him naked and in some hotel room. I saw us together, heard our laughter. It was almost too much to bear.

One of his songs came on the radio and out of the corner of my eye, I could see him nodding his head to the beat. I turned the radio off.

He cleared his throat. "This is a nice car, Chelly."

I nodded. My Mercedes *was* nice. "Well, your money bought it via the child support you pay, so thanks," I said before I could stop myself.

"I'm glad to help; you're welcome."

"Glad to help? You sure weren't glad when I had to drag you to court."

"I was stupid back then, and I was listening to people who cared more about my money than what was best for me. They've since been fired."

I glanced over at him. "Your manager?"

He nodded. "Yeah. You live and learn, and now I know better. I've surrounded myself with good people now."

I tightened my grip on the steering wheel. "Your manager told you to demand I have an abortion and then leave me in that room like a two-dollar hooker, too?"

"No, I can't blame that on anything but my own stupidity, and I apologize for saying that stuff to you, and... for leaving you there."

He sounded a little too relaxed and peaceful for my taste. "Mm-hmm, are you high, T? Because I don't want Justin exposed to that."

He shook his head, adjusted in his seat. I hated the ease he always had about himself. "I've been drug-free for years, Chelly."

"Well... good. That's not what I heard, though."

"You more than anyone should know better than to believe everything you hear."

I nodded. He was right about that. Once a tabloid reported seeing him with some newbie singer chick at some event, and I knew for a fact he didn't even attend the event. He spent the entire night with me.

"Are *you* high, Chelly? I remember you could roll a blunt like nobody's business."

"Nope, been clean and sober since the day I realized I was pregnant with Justin."

"Good."

"And *you* were the only reason I ever got involved with that stuff; you taught me how to roll blunts."

"I know. I'm sorry."

"And I don't want Justin to know about me using drugs."

"He shouldn't know, and I definitely won't tell him."

"And I don't want him hurt like I was."

"I'm not here to hurt him, Chelly. I wanna get to know him, that's all. I promise you that."

I promise you that was one of his favorite phrases. Made me shudder to hear him say it again.

As we pulled onto the school parking lot, he slipped on his shades and hat, and I silently sent up another prayer. Then I climbed out of the car and led the finest man in America into the gym. Once inside, he sat right next to me. I don't know what else I expected him to do, but it was still unnerving. We were the only parents there and I kind of wished I had someone else around to talk to.

I waved at Justin when I caught him looking in our direction. He ran to his coach and said something to him, and the next thing I knew, he was bounding up the bleachers toward us. There was no introduction needed. Justin had seen the pictures. He knew his father when he saw him. "Hey, Mom," he said.

"Hey, baby. Got a surprise for you."

"Yeah, um..." He offered T his hand. "I'm Justin."

T took his hand and smiled. I was sure those sad eyes of his were smiling, too, behind those shades. "Hi, Justin. You can call me Mateo if you'd like."

"Can I call you dad? I've never called anyone dad before." My heart ached at that statement. I wondered how T's heart was doing.

"Of course you can. I'd be honored if you did."

"Ma, can he have dinner with us? We can order pizza, right?"

My mouth dropped open. "Uh..."

"I'll pay for it—my treat," T offered.

"Uh... I thought we could eat at the manor." *Where there will be other people and maybe I won't be able to smell this man so easily because he smells like everything good I remember about him.*

"I don't wanna go there tonight, Ma, and I wanna show my dad my room and my instruments and stuff."

T grinned. "Instruments?"

Justin nodded. "Yeah."

Jesus, help me! "Okay," I acquiesced through a sigh.

"Great! Thanks, Ma! See you guys in a little bit."

"Hey, don't forget what I told you about your father visiting."

"I know. I got it, Ma."

Justin left and I almost wanted to follow him just to get away from my arch-nemesis.

"I thought he didn't know I was coming," T said.

"He didn't, not for sure."

"Then what was that about?"

I fought not to roll my eyes. "I just told him if you ever *did* visit, we'd need to keep it private, for all of our sakes."

"I see. Do people around here know he's my son? Do his friends know?"

"No."

I fixed my eyes on the basketball court. Then I thought I heard T sniffle.

"He looks like me," he said softly. "*Just* like me."

"You thought he wouldn't? Did you think he wasn't yours?" I

asked without turning to look at him.

"I never doubted that, Chelly. I knew you never cheated on me just like I never cheated on you."

"Humph," I said. But truthfully, we were joined at the hip for more than a year. If he cheated on me, I had no idea how I would've missed it.

"Um... is there a restroom nearby?" he asked in a shaky voice.

"Yeah. Right outside those doors and to the left."

He nodded. "Thanks."

He left, and I watched his butt until he disappeared through the doors. I fanned myself. Who had the heat on full blast? It wasn't that cold. I was about to burn up.

God saw me in torture and as soon as T returned, Vance entered the gym. I actually sighed and smiled for the first time that day as he climbed the bleachers, looking good in his slacks and dress shirt, sat down beside me, and kissed my cheek. "I thought that was your car out there. Watching our boy practice?"

"Yep. Um, Vance, this is Justin's father, T-uh-Mateo. Mateo, this is my fiancé, Vance."

The two men shook hands across my body.

"Pleased to meet you," Vance said. "You have an incredible son."

T nodded. "I can see that already. And you have an incredible fiancé. Congratulations."

My heart jumped for some unknown reason.

"Thanks. I still can't believe how lucky I am to have snagged this beautiful lady."

"I know the feeling," T said.

"You married?" Vance asked.

"No. I let the only woman I ever loved slip away."

Surely he wasn't talking about me. Of course he wasn't. He never really loved me. I was sure of that. He must've been talking about Rihanna or J-Lo or one of the other women I'd seen on his arm.

"But that's just life, I guess. You love and learn from the things you can't fix," T added.

"I hear you," Vance responded, and then returned his attention to me. "Dinner tonight?"

"Um, well, Mateo is having dinner with us, but you're welcome to come." *Please, come.*

"Oh, well... maybe another time. Justin needs to spend time with his dad. I'll call you." He kissed my cheek again, told T goodbye, and left.

"Nice guy," T said.

"Yeah, he's the best," I agreed.

14

"Reunion"

Justin and T got along swimmingly. I mean, it was like they were long-lost friends instead of long-lost deadbeat dad and son.

And it really irritated me.

On the ride home, Justin hammered him with questions about his music and his life. T answered them all without hesitation, even the ones about his drug use. I was glad T kept his word and didn't tell Justin about me getting high back in the day. I was pretty sure I was both high and drunk when I conceived him, but I'd never want him to know that.

At the house, I ordered the pizzas while Justin showed T his room. Minutes later, I could hear one of them playing Justin's guitar. Then I heard them both laughing, and my heart sank a little. Yeah, I was jealous. What happened to the little boy who was all mine for all those years? What happened to the anger he once had for his father? Hell, what happened to *my* anger? All I'd done since I'd laid eyes on him again was shoot a couple of weak snide remarks at him and think about our past sex life. I needed to be angry again.

The pizzas arrived, and I announced that dinner was ready.

"I woulda paid for it," T said.

"Oh, you did," I replied.

"Can me and my dad eat in my room?" Justin asked. "He was

showing me something on the guitar."

"Nope. Dad or no dad, the rules haven't changed. No eating in your room. We eat at the table, and you tell me about your day just like always."

"Sounds good to me," T said. "I'd love to hear about your day."

He was being so nice it made my skin crawl.

Well, I didn't hear a damn thing Justin said about his day, because my mind was wandering, remembering what it felt like to dig my fingers into T's thick, wavy hair and how he would sing my name when we made love. I could almost feel his hands on my body—

"Ma, you hear me?"

My head snapped up. "You say something?"

I could feel T's eyes on me, but I refused to look at him. I needed a cold shower—no, an ice bath.

"We're done. Can we go back to my room?"

"Uh-yeah."

"Need help with the dishes?" T asked.

"No, I got it."

They left and I dropped my head onto the dining room table.

***

Justin begged me into letting T stay the night. I let him sleep in the guest bedroom, and I spent the better of the night tossing and turning in my bed. And when I did manage to get in a few winks, all I saw in my dreams were images of Mateo Bridges naked, or smiling, or laughing, or in hotel rooms, or on beaches, or asleep, or doing whatever. I finally gave up around 4:00 AM and got up. I wrapped my robe around my body and headed to the kitchen to cook the one thing I could make without trouble—coffee. I was startled when I walked through the living room and heard, "Couldn't sleep either?"

It was *him*.

"Uh, no. What are you doing in here? You couldn't sleep?" Why did I ask something that had already been established? Being around this man was killing my brain cells.

"No, it's strange being here, surreal. I haven't ever spent the night under the same roof as you without us sharing a bed."

A spark shot through my lady parts. What the hell? "What?"

He stood and stepped into the light provided by the moon outside the window, and that's when I saw that he was shirtless. I pinched my arm to be sure I was awake. The pain told me I wasn't dreaming. What was going on?

"I'm sorry. Probably shouldn't have said that," he said.

"No, you shouldn't have."

"I'm just glad to be here, Chelly."

"Please call me Rochelle. Chelly died the day you left her in that hotel room in Miami."

He sighed, returned to his seat on the sofa. "Okay. Rochelle."

I walked into the kitchen but couldn't steady my trembling hands enough to make a cup of coffee if my life depended on it. So I slumped into a kitchen chair, closed my eyes, and held my head in my hands. I needed Vance. We should've already gotten married. Screw the dream wedding my mother was planning for us. We needed to get married so I could have sex and stop lusting after my ex.

Then I heard a chair move and looked up to see T sitting across from me. He was so handsome, his eyes so sad, and it made me so angry to see him sitting there. "You hurt me. I don't think you have a clue how much."

"I'm sorry. I know it's not enough, but I mean it. I'd do anything to go back in time and fix things. I was young, Chel—Rochelle. Much younger than you, and I was scared and unsure of myself. Hell, I panicked. And I was screwed up, couldn't go a whole day being sober, and although it was wrong to reject you like I did, I wasn't cut out to be a father to anyone. You know that. I probably would've screwed him up."

"What I know is that I had to come back to my hometown pregnant by a man who didn't give enough of a damn about me and his own child to even call and check on us. And you had my parents' number back then because I made sure to give it to your manager."

"He never gave it to me. I promise you that. I'm not lying. I already told you about him. That's why I got rid of him. He was always doing mess like that."

"You could've contacted me if you really wanted to, like how you started writing those letters after I spent ten years struggling to raise that boy by myself. He needed a father. He's *always* needed one."

"I wanna be that for him now."

"Now? Why now?"

"Because my head is clear."

"So you're not messed up anymore, huh?" I asked skeptically.

"No, I'm not. Five years ago I went to rehab, been clean ever since. And being clean helped me to find God and see what is really important to me. Justin is my only child; he's the only thing that matters. Not my career or even the fans, just him. Before, the drugs and booze had me numb to everything, including him. As soon as I got cleaned up, he was the first person I thought about."

I didn't have a rebuttal for that.

"I don't want to die without him knowing the real me."

I frowned, felt my stomach drop a bit. "Are you sick?"

"No, no, I'm fine. I just... I realized that I need a son as much as he needs a father. I love him, Chel—Rochelle. And I have to thank you for doing such a good job with him. He's a wonderful kid."

"I was just doing what I was supposed to do, and it wasn't easy."

"You did what I was too afraid to do, and I'm so thankful for that."

I shrugged.

"Rochelle—I... I owe you so much, and I don't know if I can ever really repay you."

I stood from the table and approached the coffeemaker again. I held my hands in front of me, and they were shaking like a weeping willow in the middle of a wind storm. I placed them on the counter and dropped my head. Then I felt him behind me. "What can I do to repay you?" he whispered.

I spun around and found myself face to face with his lips. "What?" My eyes rose to meet his.

"I asked what I can do to repay you."

Pick my chunky butt up, take me to my bed, and wear me out. "Um…"

He reached up and gently pulled at one of my braids. "I always loved your braids, baby."

Baby? "Uh… I'm fifty now." Why did I say that and what did it even mean?

"I know… exactly nine years older than me. And you look…" He leaned in and sniffed my neck. "And smell… the same. I've missed you."

"What?"

"Still got that body that I loved so much, that body that belonged to me…"

"What?"

"You are the best I've ever had."

"Huh?"

"I've missed you, Chelly," he murmured, and then he kissed me tenderly on the lips. "So much."

My knees buckled, but he caught me. "W… what?"

"I didn't come here just to make things right with my son. I came here to get you back, too. I love you. Always have. Always will."

I stood there, my heart thrashing against my ribcage. I wasn't sure what I felt, but I knew that somewhere in the back of my mind I had always wanted to hear him say those words to me, and that made me angry at myself.

So I slapped him.

Shock covered his face as he backed away from me. "Okay, I know you're angry, but—"

I slapped him again, and then I leaned in and kissed him—hard. "I'm engaged."

"Don't marry him," he replied.

"Why shouldn't I?"

"Because you love me, too."

I shook my head, stepped around him, and reclaimed my seat at the table.

He sat across from me again. "Did I buy this house, too, Chelly?"

"Yep."

"It's nice. Cozy."

"Cozy? As in much smaller than what you're used to, huh?"

"I'm over square footage. I've come to appreciate the simpler things in life."

"Hmmm, really?"

"Yeah. Hey, you remember that time we made love on the balcony of my penthouse in New York?"

I nodded, tried to swallow.

"And you screamed so loud the neighbors called the police?" he added.

"And the next day, you found out they were sub-letting and bought the penthouse right from under them, made them move out immediately."

He grinned. "And the next night we made love on *that* balcony."

"Yeah. We were high as a couple of Georgia pines."

"I wanna make love to you now that I'm sober, see if I can make you scream as loud as you did that time we were in Vegas."

Yesssss. "No."

"I'm much better. Learned some new tricks, ungraded my skills."

"I don't see how you could possibly be any better." I clamped my hand over my mouth. I hadn't meant to say that out loud.

He grinned.

"I'm not having sex with you," I said after I found my common sense again. "Hell. No."

"Why not? You obviously want to. I now know that for a fact."

"What *I* know is that I'm fifty—I know I don't look it and most of the time I don't act like it—but I *am* fifty, too old to be left holding the bag again."

"I would never do that to you again. I promise—"

"Your promises stopped meaning squat to me a long time ago, and like I said, I'm engaged."

"When's the wedding, Chelly?"

"In three months."

"So I have three months to convince you not to marry old Lance, huh?"

"*Vance*, and there's nothing you can do to convince me not to marry him."

He stood from the table, walked around to me, and bent over until his nose touched mine. He smiled at me again and then kissed me. "I bet there is."

He left the kitchen and I caught my breath.

15

"Another Round"

I took his behind back to the manor later that morning. No more sleepovers.

I had to work that day and since it was a Saturday, Justin rode along with us and hung out in his father's room, which, I found out, had been changed to Room Ten. I smelled a Rosa plot all over that one, but since he had already declared his love for me, I didn't think it made much of a difference what room he was in. And it didn't make a difference what he said, or how he flashed those brown eyes at me, or how sad they were, or how sexy his voice and body were. I was not giving in to him. No way.

Never.

"Hey, girl," Dee Dee said, peeking her head in my office door.

I looked up and groaned inwardly. I was in no mood for an interrogation, especially knowing he was on a twisted mission to win me back. So I said, "Hey" rather unenthusiastically.

"I heard he spent the night with you last night." Well, that was direct and to the point.

"You heard?"

"Okay, I assumed."

"Dee Dee, I really can't right now."

"Okay, okay, I just wanted to tell you I found you in some pics."

She moved closer to my desk, whipped out her phone, and held it in front of me. I took it and swiped through the pictures. I hadn't seen those in a long time—us holding hands stepping out of a limo, us entering and leaving different clubs and restaurants, both of us always with shades covering our eyes. I had a figure to die for back then. Those pictures brought back a lot more memories, most of which were good ones. I smiled and handed her phone back to her.

"So…" she prodded.

"So… what?"

"How is it seeing him again?"

I rubbed my forehead and looked up at her. "To be honest, it's hard. We didn't part on good terms."

"Yeah, I figured you two had a bad break-up since you never mentioned him before."

I nodded.

"Well, now you have Vance."

"Right."

"I mean, he's no Teo B, but he's a good guy."

"Dee Dee…"

"Okay, I'm gone."

After she left, I closed my door and took a nap at my desk.

Rosa had to come wake me up for lunch. "Didn't get any sleep last night?" she asked.

"How could I with him in my house?"

"Well, I know you're mad at the man, but what did he do last night? He seems so nice and—"

"He declared his love for me, says he wants me back."

Her eyes widened. "Oh... what did you say?"

"No! I said no! What do you think I said?"

"That you love him back."

"Why would I say that?"

"Because you do, sugar. Anyone can see that."

I scoffed. "How so?"

"Well, the evidence is in the fact that you haven't had a real relationship since you left him."

"I have Vance."

"You don't love Vance."

"I'll learn to love him."

"No, you won't."

I stood and squeezed past her out the door. "I'm not going to sit there and listen to this. I'ma go eat."

"The truth is hard to hear, isn't it?"

I rolled my eyes as I made my way to the dining room. Lunch was peaceful since T didn't eat with us, but dinner? That was a different story. I arrived to see my son and his father sitting side by side at the table. T jumped up when he saw me walk into the dining room and offered to fix my plate for me. I declined, fixed my own plate, and sat as far away from him as I possibly could. I was busy cutting into my country fried steak when he and Justin moved to my end of the table and flanked me. "You didn't have to move," I said to Justin.

"Dad said we should all sit together," he replied with a grin on his face, and at that moment, I knew T had taken the gloves off and enlisted our son's help in his insane mission. *Bastard.*

"I see," I said and did my best to ignore T and Rosa and Dee Dee, who were all grinning like some fools.

"Hey, everyone! Sorry I'm late."

It was Vance. I had invited him to dinner, and he'd said he'd try to make it. I was so happy to see him, I jumped up from the table and rushed to him, wrapping my arms around him.

He kissed me. "Nice greeting."

"Hey, Vance. Help yourself," Ms. Rosa said.

"Thanks, Ms. Rosa."

I reclaimed my seat, and with a lowered voice, asked T if he could move down a seat to make room for Vance.

His reply was, "Nope."

I sighed and tried to stand so that I could move when I felt a hand squeeze my thigh, and then T whispered, "Remember that night in Vegas? The tub?"

I remembered, all right, and just the thought of that night made my temperature rise. I suddenly couldn't move a muscle.

"You still sleep naked, baby? I do," he murmured.

I grabbed my water and guzzled it.

"Hey, Vance!" T said a little too cheerily. "Why don't you come sit next to me, let me get to know my son's future stepfather?"

Vance gave me a slightly confused look. "Uh... sure."

The whole time T chatted it up with Vance, he kept squeezing my thigh under the table. And if he wasn't squeezing it, he was rubbing it. And my fool self let him because it felt *soooo good.* His was the last touch like that I'd felt from a man, and it felt so familiar and I hated myself for loving it. I was a soggy mess by the end of the meal. But when he moved his hand up to my cookie jar, I slipped my fork under the table and poked his hand. He jerked it away, and I smiled.

After I walked Vance to his car, told Justin to wait in mine, and made sure the coast was clear, I went to Room Ten and knocked on the door. T opened it, and when he saw me, his thin lips parted and his wide mouth spread into a smile. I pushed past him and entered the room, tried to ignore the fact that he was only wearing a pair of boxers. "You sure stripped quick," I said.

He moved closer to me. "I must've subconsciously known you'd come."

I raised my hand. "I just came to tell you that if you pull some mess like you did at dinner again, I'm going to come in here and castrate your half-Puerto Rican behind while you sleep. I have access to the master key."

"Man, I've missed you."

I tried to leave. He stopped me by grasping my arm.

"Let me go, T," I demanded.

"I love you and I'ma get you back. No way am I gonna let you marry that lame dude."

"T, we've been apart for fifteen years. I could've been married twice by now. What made you think you had any chance of coming here and getting me back?"

"The fact that I love you just as much today as I did fifteen years ago, actually more now that I've seen you again and touched you again. I still remember every inch of your body. I remember everything about you. I need to make things up to you, because no one has ever made me as happy as you did. Believe me, Chelly, as mad as you are at me, I'm even angrier at myself for hurting you."

I shook my head. "T..."

"Justin invited me to church tomorrow. I'll meet you at your house. I think I know the way there." He leaned in and kissed my cheek. "I'll see you in the morning, baby."

I left, telling myself that I was going to have to have a talk with Justin.

***

My son lied to me, or at least I didn't believe him when he said he and his father didn't discuss me. I asked him if he was still okay with me and Vance getting married, and he said yes. Then I asked him what he thought about his father.

He said, "He's great!"

I could have thrown up all over my own car at that moment.

"So, you're not mad at him anymore?" I asked.

He shook his young, naive head. "No, he apologized and explained everything."

"What did he explain?"

"That he was really young and scared but that he loved me and you a lot. And that he wished he could change things in the past."

"I thought y'all didn't talk about me."

"That's all he said, that he loved you and still does."

"That's it, you sure?"

"Yeah."

"You believe him?"

"Yeah, he cried about it."

"Cried?" Boy, was he laying it on thick. I mean, he could probably cry on cue. He'd been in a couple of movies and was a half-decent actor.

"Yeah."

"Hmm. So you forgive him that easily?"

"Yeah, ain't that what I'm supposed to do? You always say I should listen in church, and I hear the pastor talking about forgiving people all the time. He says we have to forgive others if we expect God to forgive us."

Ouch.

"My dad said he cleared his calendar. He's gonna be here for a couple of months."

"What?! I mean, what?"

"And he wants to take us to see his house in LA."

"Us?"

"Yeah, he said he didn't expect you to let me go with him alone. We can go, right?"

"Uh, I don't know when we'd have time. You have school and—"

"He said we could do it one weekend, promised to have me back in time for school."

"Promised—we'll see, Justin. We'll see."

16

"Smooth Criminal"

"Scoot over," I hissed at T, who was darn near sitting on top of me on the church pew.

He scooted over about a micrometer. "The meaner you are to me, the more I love you."

"You look crazy sitting up in here with those shades on."

"You want me to take them off?"

"Lord, no. I don't have time for that pandemonium."

He flashed me a smile and I groaned, wishing Vance was there with me. Of all days to decide to visit his mother's church, he picked this one.

"Did Justin tell you about my invitation to my house?"

"Yes, and the answer is no."

"Oh..."

He sounded disappointed, but I didn't care.

"I have him a room set up and everything. I hate he won't get to see it, but you're the boss."

"Did you tell him about the room?"

"Yeah."

I sighed and was thankful when the youth choir, including my boy, began to sing. Justin led a song, and I thought T would jump out of his seat with pride. He sounded a lot like his father. Okay, he sounded *just* like him. I always knew that but tried to block that fact out. T was just thrilled to discover this. I half-expected him to secure the boy a record deal before the service ended.

"He's so good!" he gushed, with a big cheesy grin on his face. "Reminds me so much of myself."

I nodded. "Yeah, he's very talented. Can play several instruments, too. All self-taught."

He looked like he was going to explode with joy.

And as crazy as it sounds, I think my pastor was in on T's conspiracy, standing up there preaching about forgiveness and second chances. Really? He couldn't think of anything else to preach about? I was so glad when church was over. My parents had invited T to Sunday dinner, and I knew they'd have my back.

***

I am related to a pack of Judases.

Even my daddy seemed to like T. My *daddy*. Mama spent the evening giggling all over herself. Daddy gave him an extra piece of chicken, and he never did that! I already knew Justin was a lost cause.

After dinner, I sat in a corner of the living room and stared at the foolishness that unfolded. My parents knew my story, how I struggled to get over this man and struggled to raise my son alone. And there they were, skinning and grinning in his face—star-struck. Mama even cornered me in the bathroom and asked me to take pictures of his house when Justin and I went to visit.

"We aren't going. Who said we were going?"

"Teo said it, and Justin is so excited. Oh, he's going to be so disappointed if he doesn't get to go."

"Well, I was disappointed when *Teo* refused to help me raise him."

"Lord, you and that unforgiving spirit…"

"Some things are unforgivable, Mama."

"Says who? Because Jesus said the only unforgiveable sin is blaspheming against the Holy Spirit."

"He probably did that, too."

"Rochelle, you need to stop."

"Look, I ain't Jesus."

"Good thing, or else we'd all be doomed. You're not hurting anyone but yourself harboring those feelings for him. It's a wonder you don't have a head full of gray hair, holding on to all that hatred. He was young. Shoot, I didn't realize just how young he was. You were older and more mature, Rochelle."

I frowned. "So everything is *my* fault?"

"No, it's just that knowing he was so young puts a different spin on things. I didn't realize before how big of an age difference there is between you two."

"He was twenty-five, not *five*, when he got me pregnant. He was a man, man enough to make Justin, and even though I was thirty-four when I got pregnant, thirty-five when I had him, I was scared and inexperienced, too. But I did what I had to do. He should've stepped up and that's all there is to it."

"Isn't that what he's trying to do now?"

"It's been fifteen years, Mama."

"I know, honey, but Justin has been waiting for this for a long time. Just do this for him, okay?"

That next Friday, I found myself aboard Teo B's private jet, on my way to sunny damn LA.

17

"Bloodstream"

Someone, one of my traitors, must've told T my favorite color was yellow, because my temporary room in his sprawling home was decorated in various shades of yellow from the walls to the duvet on the bed. Two dozen yellow roses were crammed into a lovely crystal vase on the bedside table. Even the adjoining bathroom was yellow. The room was beautiful, as was the entire house, really tranquil and peaceful. I had to remind myself that I hated this man.

And Justin's room? A teenager's fantasy complete with video games, a huge flat screen TV, and a balcony that overlooked the Olympic-sized backyard. He even gave Justin his favorite guitar. I remembered him writing songs with it when we were together. He'd named it Chelly 2, said she was his second favorite girl.

I sighed and tried to pull myself off of my little walk down memory lane. Two days. I could make it two days under the same roof with him. And as soon as I made it back home, I was going to call Vance and tell him to screw the big wedding. I was going to convince him to elope, because if I was married, maybe I'd stop wanting to have sex with T.

I knelt beside the soft bed and prayed: *Dear Lord, please give me strength. Take these feelings I have for T that I can't seem to get rid of away, and make me love Vance. Please, Lord. I know you can do it. In Jesus' name, Amen.*

As I stood to my feet, T entered the room.

"You can't knock?" I huffed.

"Sorry, I'm usually here alone so knocking isn't required."

I sat on the foot of the bed. "I guess Rihanna doesn't care if you intrude on her, huh?"

He moved closer, stood right in front of me. "I told you on the plane that I was never with her. She's too young. I prefer more mature women… like you."

"And like J-Lo?"

He shrugged. "She's a friend. I wanna be more than friends with you."

"Madonna?"

"Come on, now. Be serious. You know she ain't got the kind of body I like…. but you do."

"Humph. Still sleeping with groupies?"

He tilted his head to the side. "When have you ever known me to sleep with groupies?"

I lifted an eyebrow and gave him a skeptical look.

He sighed. "Okay, okay… I did sleep with a few, but that was before we got together."

"And after…"

"Okay… and after, but I haven't been with anyone since I got out of rehab."

"Really? No one?"

"No one. As soon as I got my mind clear, I could only think of you."

"So I don't need to worry about your woman busting up in here and jumping on me?"

"No, because I don't have a woman. I told you that on the plane, too. I'm talking to the only woman I want right now."

"Mm-hmm."

There was a moment of silence. Then he said, "Justin likes his room."

"I know. What boy his age wouldn't?"

"Do you like yours, baby?"

"Don't call me that, and yes, it's a nice room."

"I had it decorated for you years ago, remembered how you liked yellow when we were together."

"You sure Justin didn't tell you that?"

He shook his head and squatted in front of me. "I told you, I remember everything about you. Yeah, I was high a lot, but I wasn't in a coma. You meant the world to me, Chelly. Still do."

"Rochelle."

"Old boy can call you that if he wants, but you'll always be my Chelly."

"Why he gotta be old?"

"I've seen his clothes. Looks like a high school principal."

"That's what he is."

"I know."

"Everyone's not rich, T."

"You don't have to be rich to have style." He stood and walked over to the vase of roses. "There are more of these for you in my room."

"Pity I won't get to see them."

"What's stopping you?"

"The high school principal."

He nodded. "Well, if you change your mind, I'm right across the hall, love."

He walked back over to me, lifted my chin, and kissed me deeply. Once our lips had parted, I said, "I really hate you."

He grinned. "See you at dinner."

He left, and I fell back on the bed. How could a pair of jogging pants look so sexy on any man? How could a kiss make me want to climb the walls? I turned over, buried my face in the duvet, and let out a muffled scream. My prayer hadn't worked.

***

Dinner was good. He ordered about ten pizzas, every type you could imagine from buffalo chicken to vegan. He was spoiling Justin already, and I didn't like it. I was going to have to pull him aside and tell him to slow down, but pulling him aside could've easily led to something else and I knew I was weak when it came to him, very weak, unfortunately. I started thinking that maybe I should've slept around after we broke up so the memories of us being intimate wouldn't be so vivid, and maybe I wouldn't be so easily aroused by him. But that was a stupid notion, too. I wouldn't have wanted to set that example for Justin.

After dinner, T and Justin went into T's in-house studio and started a little jam session. I sat in a chair in the corner and watched, and in thirty minutes' time, the two had actually written a song together. He recorded it and evidently sent Justin a copy on his phone or something. I had no idea how all of that worked, but it sounded good. Next thing I knew, Justin was racing out of the room, calling all of his friends. That was when I realized people back home were going to know who his father was when we returned and that really worried me. I was deep in thought with a furrowed brow when T approached me. "I'm so glad I got to share this with him. I'm so glad he loves music."

"Yeah, he's just as excited as I remember you would get back in the day when you'd write a new song. You'd sing it for me. I always loved that."

"Yeah... we had some good times, Chelly. Some of the best times of my life."

"Yeah, we did," I admitted.

We were silent until I released a sigh.

"What's wrong? Why're you looking like that? You don't like the song?" T queried.

"No, I love it. It's a great song. I was just thinking... nothing will be the same for him again now. Nothing will be normal. He's on the phone telling his friends that he just made a song with his dad and he'll probably tell them who you are, and I can't blame him. You are... *you*, after all. But what if the paparazzi get wind of who he is to you and where he lives? What if we get home and people are crowded outside our house just like they're outside your gate right now? I never really had to worry about any of that before."

"That's why you never went to the media about me, isn't it, why you never told anyone he was my son? You were protecting Justin."

I frowned. "Is that what you expected me to do? Go to the media and tell them you were a deadbeat to your son?"

"It's what any other woman would've done, and rightfully so, I suppose."

"I'm not any other woman."

"Yeah, I know," he said quietly.

I sighed. "I just want Justin to lead a normal life."

He grabbed a chair, dragged it next to mine, and sat in it. "Okay... look, I don't want to cause him any trouble, but I can't lie. All of that stuff you just said about the paparazzi will probably happen if news of who he is gets out. There are perks to being associated with me; there are also inconveniences. But you already knew that. What I can do is make sure he's as safe as possible, him and you."

"Thank you."

"But of course that would be easier if we were a family, the three of us living under the same roof and you in my bed, and—"

I chuckled. "Wow. I can't believe I didn't see that coming. I have a life, T. A nice, peaceful life. And I ain't shacking up with you."

"Who said anything about shacking up? I'm tryna wife you, baby. And are you going to sit there and tell me you didn't enjoy our time together? You didn't enjoy that lifestyle at all?"

"I have a kid. *We* have a kid. That lifestyle wouldn't work now."

"I'm not saying things have to be as erratic as they were in the past. We can live in that little town of yours if you want. It'll just take some extra security. But we can still travel. I just wanna make you happy."

"Then leave me alone."

"I can't, because that wouldn't make either of us happy."

I shook my head and stood to leave. He hopped out of his chair and swiftly pulled me into his arms. Then he kissed me as he held me so tightly I could barely breathe… and I kissed him back, and then I wrapped my leg around his waist, and then I started unbuckling his belt, and then I heard a noise that shook us apart. We both turned to see Justin standing in the doorway with a huge grin on his face.

"Sorry," he said. "I'll leave you two alone."

"No—" I began.

"Yes, we'll see you in a second, son," T interrupted me.

Justin nodded, that grin still on his face as he turned and left the room.

"How the hell are we going to explain this?" I asked, disgusted with myself.

"What's to explain? We're his parents. We made him. He knows we've done it before."

I slumped back into my seat. "Oh, Lord. Please help me."

"I love you so much, Chelly. You love me, too, don't you?"

"I cannot stand you!"

"You don't mean that, not really. I can feel it in your kisses, your touch. You love me."

I shook my head.

"What do you want me to do? What do I need to say to make you forgive me and take me back?" He dropped to his knees. "I'm begging you to please forgive me and stop being angry with me. I'm sorry. But can't you see that by hurting you, I hurt myself? I missed out on fifteen years of seeing my son grow up and being with the love of my life. *Fifteen years*. I love you, baby. Can you forgive me and learn to love me again? Please, *please*, baby."

I looked down at the handsome face that would make any woman's heart skip a few beats. "You don't understand."

"Yes, I do. I understand that I messed up, *bad*. I wish I had been man enough to do the right thing, make you my wife, be a father to… to our son, but I wasn't then. I am now, Chelly, and I will crawl around this house, outside if you want, groveling for your forgiveness. I'll take out a full page ad in all the papers admitting that I've been a damn fool. I'll pull a Robin Thicke and write a whole album for you. Hell, every love song I've written since the day I met you is about you anyway. I will do *anything*. Just name it. Whatever it takes for me to fix things, I'll do it. I need you, Chelly. I'll do anything to get you back."

"You think everything is about you, don't you? This is not about you! I'm angrier at myself than anyone! I'm angry at myself and I can't forgive myself for loving you all these years and for missing you and needing you and wanting you! You treated me like crap, left me in that room like an old beat-up suitcase, and I *still* love you! I have not been with another man since you! Absolutely no sex in fifteen years! You know how pathetic that is? Loving someone who stabbed you in the heart? Being true to them against your own will? I hate myself for being so weak for you. I wanna crawl in your bed right now! What kind of woman keeps loving the man who destroyed her life? A damn fool one, that's what kind.

"I remember what your favorite song is, that you hate mayonnaise, that you like your bacon soft—not crispy, that your first girlfriend's name was Angela, that you wrote your first song when you were in the fifth grade, and a whole bunch of other random stuff you can't find on some fan website. I remember how it feels to be in your arms, how it feels to… to—you are in my head and I can't get you out and I hate myself for it. It's like you are a part of my DNA or something, like you're in my bloodstream, like a drug or a disease or… God, help me!"

His sad eyes were glued to me. "A d… disease?"

I looked down at my trembling hands and then back at him. "You're all over me. You… I can't shake you loose. I can't… *I can't*…" A single tear rolled down my face.

He reached up and wiped the tear away with his hand. "Baby… I—"

I groaned. "I'm just too damn old for this!"

"Chelly, baby, don't you see I'm in the same predicament? You're in my blood, my DNA. I can't shake *you* loose. We belong together. Can't you see that? That's the only way either of us will be happy."

I held my head in my hands. "No-no! Look, T, I need to marry Vance and learn to love him. I need to let you go, because I know you're just going to hurt me and I can't survive another blow like the last one you gave me. *I can't.* If I let you hurt me like that again, I'll die. I wanted to die before, and truthfully, Justin was the only thing that kept me going. I never want to feel that pain again in my life. I need you to understand that. And if you really love me, you'll leave me alone. Please, just let it go."

This time when I stood to leave, he didn't stop me.

Later that night, when I felt him climb into bed with me, I flipped over, ready to cuss him completely out, thinking to myself that I should've locked my door. Then I remembered I was in *his* house and was sure his persistent ass had a key.

"I just wanna hold you, just for a little while. I got you earlier, heard you loud and clear. I messed up, I know I did, but I love you and I can't help that. I need to hold you, baby. That's all, I promise. I'll leave before Justin wakes up."

I don't know why, but I nodded and turned my back to him. Shirtless and in only a pair of pajama bottoms, he spooned himself behind me and rested his arm on my waist. I closed my eyes and quietly sighed as he kissed my shoulder, caressed my arm, pressed his body against mine, whispered, "I love you so much, Chelly. I know you don't believe me. I know *why* you don't believe me. But I do love you. You're the only woman I have ever loved."

He scooted down and kissed my back. "I love you, baby, and I'm so sorry."

I held my breath, blinked back tears.

"I love you," he whispered over and over again. "I always will. I don't care who you marry, I will always love you and I will never forgive myself for hurting you. *Never.*"

I let my tears fall in silence.

And then this man, this gorgeous man, buried his face in my hair and wept, his body racking with sobs.

When his tears ended, he whispered, "I breathe for you, Chelly. I really do. I breathe for you, baby. You're everything to me."

It felt like Heaven—all of it, being in his arms, feeling his touch, hearing his voice, and a couple of hours later, when he climbed out of bed leaving the space beside me warm and empty, I wished more than anything that he'd stayed.

18

"Matrimony: Maybe You"

The rest of the trip was pretty uneventful for me, because I faked an illness and spent the next day in my room while T and Justin gallivanted around LA or made music together in the studio. T didn't bother me anymore except for the bouquet of yellow roses he delivered to me with a get-well card attached. He looked so pitiful and helpless that I almost felt sorry for him.

Almost.

I was so relieved when we finally made it back to Hyacinth Valley. The first thing I did was call Vance and tell him I wanted to elope—ASAP. He went right along with it. I think he was ready to skip the preliminaries and get to the honeymoon. So was I, because spending so much time around T had my loins on fire.

He set everything up with a justice of the peace in Paxton, and we made plans to wed that very week, on that Friday. We'd honeymoon in Little Rock and be back on Monday to resume our normal lives. I didn't tell anyone anything except that we were taking a little trip over the weekend. My parents would watch Justin when he wasn't hanging out at Hyacinth Manor with his father.

"So you need to be off Friday, too?" Ms. Rosa asked.

"Yeah, is that a problem? We don't have anything planned, do we?"

"Well, the only upcoming event is Dorcas's engagement party, and I need to start interviewing cooks to replace her since she and Farris are planning to travel after they get married. I was counting on your help for both projects."

"Well, I can help when I get back next week."

"I guess. Something doesn't feel right about you taking this trip, sugar. It doesn't set well in my spirit."

"You think we're gonna have a wreck or something?" I knew Ms. Rosa's spirit, and it didn't lie. She truly had a gift.

"I don't know, but I know without a doubt that you shouldn't take this trip."

I frowned. "Well, all the plans have been made…"

"Just pray about it, sugar. Maybe you two can postpone it. Something just doesn't feel right about this."

I nodded.

***

I was a nervous wreck as I drove Justin to school that Friday morning. I hadn't heeded Ms. Rosa's warning. I needed to do this for my sanity. I would deal with any fall-out or repercussions later.

"Ma, you okay?" Justin asked with concern in his voice.

I nodded. "I'm fine, baby."

"You don't look like it."

"Just tired, I guess. Are you okay? I mean, you still enjoying spending time with your dad?"

"Yeah… I guess."

I glanced over at him. "Something wrong? He do something?" If he hurt my baby's feelings, I was going to hurt *him*, so help me God.

"He's just been… sad."

"Sad? Why?"

"He says it's because he can't figure out how to make you happy."

I sighed. There he went using my son against me again. "I'm happy, Justin. Don't worry about me, and your father will be okay."

"He keeps crying about it."

I didn't know what to say, so I didn't say anything. But this was the cryingest man…

"I really think he loves you, Ma."

"You want us to get back together, Justin?"

"I think it'd be cool."

"But you know I'm marrying Vance, honey. I thought you liked him."

"I do, but he's not my dad."

Dang.

"Well… I'm sorry things can't be the way you want them. I wouldn't be happy with your dad."

"But you'll be happy with Mr. Washington?"

I nodded my lie.

"As long as you're happy, I'm good."

I dropped him off in front of the school, then headed back to Hyacinth Valley to Vance's house. He'd taken the day off, too.

When I pulled into his driveway, I felt so queasy, I was sure I was going to throw up all over his front door as I rang the doorbell.

"There she is, the bride to be," he said as he opened the door and let me in. He looked handsome wearing a fresh haircut, a crisp white dress shirt, and black slacks that fit him almost too well.

"Good morning," I replied.

He kissed my cheek. "Almost ready. Have a seat in the living room."

I sat there on his nice sofa and rubbed my sweaty hands on the cushion and adjusted my white dress a million times. I combed my fingers through my braids and took deep breaths and choked back bile. By the time he announced he was ready to go, I was nearly totally unhinged.

The ride to the justice of the peace was eerily silent, and he was driving so doggone slow! I wanted to yell at him to put some pep in it, but that was Vance—safe, sensible, secure. The exact opposite of Mateo Bridges, who was spontaneous and reckless, and for me, the antithesis of security. But I loved him. There was no sense in denying that. But I was still marrying Vance. I had to.

We made it to the justice of the peace's house on time and held hands as we approached the door. Vance rang the doorbell and my heart thudded in my chest. The door opened to reveal a stocky older black man with a bald head and bowed legs. He wore an olive green suit and a bright smile. "You two must be the love birds—Chance and Rotel. I'm George Donaldson."

Vance glanced at me. "Uh, Vance and Rochelle. Here's our

marriage license, Mr. Donaldson," he said, handing the document to him.

"Mm-hmm, well, y'all come on in. Got the living room set up for you. My daughter's going to be the witness. Maydell! They here!"

I jumped when he yelled for his daughter. Vance squeezed my hand.

The living room walls were covered with tiny Christmas lights, and there was a preacher's podium set up in the middle. My hands shook as Vance and I took our places in front of the podium. Maydell, who was just as wide as she was tall, stood to the side in a floral-print dress and wiped tears from her eyes like me and Vance were her closest and dearest friends.

I gave Vance a nervous smile and then turned to face Mr. Donaldson. As soon as he spoke the words, "We are gathered here today," I vomited all over that podium.

19

"You"

I sat in my bedroom, naked, trying to figure out what to do next. I'd left poor Vance at the altar. Well, that's not entirely true. He did have to drive me home, and I tried my best to explain why I couldn't marry him. But my words were jumbled and I was sure he thought I was insane. And the look in his eyes broke my heart, and his having to drive through the throng of reporters who'd gotten wind of where Teo B's son lived didn't help the situation. He'd asked if it was because of T, and rather than lie, I told him yes. *Everything* was because of him. Vance was probably going to hate me forever for dumping him not once, but twice, and I couldn't even blame him.

"Lord, all I wanted to do was find someone for me and a father for Justin. That's all. But I can't stop loving T. He is all I've thought about since the day I met him," I said.

Then a light bulb popped on in my head, and I sat there for a few more minutes before jumping in the shower and getting dressed.

After gathering myself, I called the manor and asked Rosa to come and pick me up since my car was still at Vance's house. She did, and thankfully, she didn't question me on the way back to the manor. Once we arrived, I bounded up the stairs and knocked on his door. When he opened it, I ignored the fact that he was once again shirtless.

"Where's Justin?" I asked.

"Uh, wasn't your mother picking him up from school today? She hasn't brought him here yet."

"There are a million paparazzi at my house."

He frowned. "What? Let me make some calls and—"

"No. Sit down."

"Uh, o… okay."

I straddled his lap and kissed him for a long, lingering moment.

He gave me a surprised look as he wrapped his arms around me. "Damn, um… thank you?"

I stood in front of him and blurted, "I wanted a husband for me and a father for Justin and I was so tired of being alone and I thought Vance would work, but…"

"But, he didn't work?"

"He *couldn't* work, because I can't seem to stop loving *you*. I've tried, and I can't. I'm not fit for anyone else, and if I don't have sex with you soon, I'm going to explode. So I guess we need to go ahead and do this."

He smiled. "Do this?"

"Get together, be together, whatever. I guess it was supposed to be you all along."

"I'm glad you finally realized that."

I rolled my eyes. "Look, we can move to LA or whatever if Justin is okay with it, but I'm not shacking up with you, Mateo Bridges."

"Baby, I already told you I want you to be my wife. I'll marry you today, right this minute if you want to." He stood, pulled me into his arms, and kissed my neck.

"I ain't signing no pre-nup, T."

"I don't want you to. I'm never letting you leave me. I'm locking you down for good, putting some handcuffs on your mean butt. Clink-clink, baby."

"What if we can't be together sober?" I asked.

"Well, one thing's for damn sure, we're both miserable apart and sober. I say we give it a chance, baby. Look, I've prayed about this and I know you have, too. We belong together."

"Okay, I know you're right. I'm just… scared."

"I know. So am I, but I gotta be with you."

He lifted my shirt and tried to pull me toward the bed.

"Un-uh, no cookies without a ring. I don't need a big wedding or anything, but we're gonna have to take vows before we have sex. I deserve it—hell, I've *earned* it."

He released me and walked over to the closet, dug around in one of his suitcases, and returned with a ring box. When he opened it, I gasped. It was a beautiful square-cut yellow diamond surrounded by smaller white diamonds with a platinum band. "I bought this when Justin and I went shopping in LA, hoping you'd change your mind. He helped me pick it out."

"It's beautiful, T! Justin knows about this and didn't tell me?"

"I asked him not to. Your mom and dad know about it, too. Gave me their blessing."

I shook my head. "Of course they did."

"Take that dude's ugly-ass ring off so I can put this one on you."

Poor Vance. He was a good man, but the ring he gave me *was* ugly.

"Is that how you're proposing?"

He lowered himself onto one knee, reached for my hand. "I'm sorry this took fifteen years, but Rochelle Warrior, would you do me the honor of becoming my wife?"

"T, if you hurt me like you did before, I'ma make good on my threat to cut off your half-Puerto Rican balls."

"Do you know how long I've prayed for this? Hell, if I mess this up, I'll *help* you cut 'em off. If I'm that big of a damn fool, I don't deserve to keep 'em."

I took a deep breath and released it. "Okay, ask me again."

"Will you marry me?" he repeated.

I looked into those eyes of his. "Let me think about it—yes."

He grinned, slipped the ring on my finger, stood up, and kissed me. "Now let's get married so we can come back and try this bed out. We need to get a license before the place closes. I know everything closes early in these little towns."

"Um, we have a little problem that I guess kind of slipped my mind."

His shoulders sagged. "What is it?"

"I already have a marriage license with Vance. We were going to get married today."

"Oh, that's not a problem. We'll just take it back."

"What if they won't give me another one so soon?"

"I have a jet, love. As long as you're not legally married, we can go get married anywhere."

I grinned. "Well, let's go so you can show me your new tricks."

"Your wish is my command, baby. I'm gonna give you everything I should've given you over these past fifteen years and more."

20

"...Til the Cops Come Knockin'"

He was right. He *was* even better than before. Shoot, he was better than better.

And from all the noise he made, so was I.

As we lay side by side in our Las Vegas suite, I stared into the darkness and thanked the good Lord over and over again. I loved this man more than I even realized, and if I was honest with myself, I would have to admit that I always had and always would.

I rolled over and peered at him. "You're going to get us kicked out with all that hollering. Looks like the tables have turned with us."

"First of all, this is a penthouse suite and there's no one else on this floor. Second of all, I was singing, not *hollering*," he said breathily.

"Hmmm, I never knew you could sing in the whistle register..."

He wrapped his arm around me. "You trying to be funny, baby? It's not like *you* were silent."

"Whatever. I wasn't screaming like *you*."

"Yet."

"Yet, huh?"

"Yeah, I haven't pulled all of my tricks out of my bag, girl."

I frowned as I lifted my head. "What you waiting on?"

"Oh, you ready for more?"

"After fifteen years? Heck, yeah!"

"I'm about to wear you out!" He ducked his head under the covers.

"Hey, T-baby?"

He peeked up at me. "Yeah, love?"

"I love you."

He scooted up in the bed and kissed me deeply. "I love you, too, baby. I promise you that."

Epilogue

Rosa

Two months later...

Lord, have mercy! Dorcas's engagement party was something else! I was so glad Rochelle and Teo were able to come back for it. He even sang a couple of songs, and let me tell you, he brought the house down! That man has a voice on him!

But as happy as I was for her, everyone around me falling in love and getting engaged or married was messing with my business. First I had to replace August, and now I'd have to find someone to take Rochelle's place since she'd moved to California, and I still hadn't found a replacement for Dorcas.

I guess I had a lot on my mind that night. I was happy for everyone, just a little stressed, and maybe I had one too many cocktails, because I somehow lost my way to my room and ended up here—in Room Ten.

Bonus Tracks:

"Shame" Tyrese

"Can't Get Over You" Maze featuring Frankie Beverly

"Foolish Heart" Steve Perry

For information about support groups for single parents, visit:

http://www.singleandparenting.org/

For information about and help for alcohol and/or drug addiction, visit:

http://www.aa.org/ or http://www.recovery.org/

For more information about Adrienne Thompson, visit:

http://adriennethompsonwrites.webs.com

Sign up for Adrienne's newsletter here:

http://eepurl.com/jnDmH

Follow Adrienne on Twitter!

https://twitter.com/A_H_Thompson

Like Adrienne on Facebook!

https://www.facebook.com/AdrienneThompsonWrites

Join Adrienne's Facebook group!!

https://www.facebook.com/groups/674088779363625/

Follow Adrienne on Pinterest!

http://www.pinterest.com/ahthompsn/

Connect with Adrienne on Goodreads!

https://www.goodreads.com/author/show/5051327.Adrienne_Thompson

Also by Adrienne Thompson

The *Bluesday* Series:

Bluesday

Lovely Blues

Blues In The Key Of B

Locked out of Heaven (Tomeka's Story – A Bluesday
Continuation)

The *Been So Long* Series:

Rapture (A Been So Long Prequel)

If (Wasif's Story) A Been So Long Prequel

Been So Long

Little Sister (Cleo's Story—a companion novel to Been So Long)

Been So Long 2 (Body and Soul)

Been So Long III (Whatever It Takes)

SEPTEMBER (The Christina Dandridge Story—a Been So Long
companion novel)

The *Your Love Is King* Series:

Your Love Is King

Better

The *Ain't Nobody* Series:

Sedução (Seduction)—an Ain't Nobody Prequel

Ain't Nobody

The Latter Rain Series:

After the Pain

No Pain, No Gain

Stand-alone novels:

Home

See Me

When You've Been Blessed (Feels Like Heaven)

Summertime (A Novella)

Nonfiction Titles:

Just Between Us (Inspiring Stories by Women) –as a contributor

Seven Days of Change (A Flash Devotional)

Poetry:

Poetry from the Soul… for the Soul, Volume II

All books are available at amazon.com, barnesandnoble.com, and kobobooks.com

Please enjoy this excerpt from *Joy and Pain* (Latter Rain: Book III) Coming March 2016:

Rosa

One thing life has taught me is that things happen in their own time, and often, that time is not the time you expected. I met Lawrence Noble when I least expected it. I was a school teacher back then. Not because it had been some dream of mine to teach, but because I was a young black woman who grew up in the country, and that was the only option I saw for myself in the early seventies. Nevertheless, I grew to enjoy my job and love my kindergarten students. Lawrence was the father of one of my students. He was also married.

I was fresh out of school—just twenty-two when we met. Lawrence was thirty and handsome. He owned a local gas station and a couple more in neighboring towns. I'm not going to sit here and lie and say I fell in love with him, because I didn't.

I fell in *lust*.

And three months after our little affair began, I found out I was pregnant with our child, a little boy I'd name Freeman Stark—Man for short. Those were the old days, and my little hometown was the buckle of the Bible belt, so I was scorned by the community, lost my job, and eventually left Hyacinth Valley. I didn't return for several years. The older folks that had looked down on me were mostly gone by the time I did return. So were Lawrence and his family. Man was all grown up, and I was a mature woman with second sight and enough life experiences to fill three or four books, but I had never been in love.

And to be honest, I had no desire to ever be in love. No desire at all…